"You sit," she told him. "I'll ride."

The blonde raised her arms overhead, stretching, writhing on Nanos's lap like a wounded snake. Then her fingers touched the side of her headband and something bright and impossibly thin slithered out from under the terry cloth and snapped taut between her hands.

The strand of stainless steel was around the Greek's neck before he could get his hands up, slicing into the skin of his throat like a razor, cutting off his air as if by a switch.

"Die, bastard!" she cried.

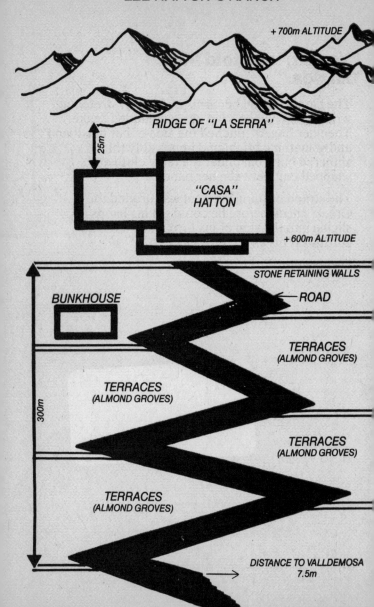

LEE HATTON'S RANCH

+ 700m ALTITUDE

RIDGE OF "LA SERRA"

25m

"CASA" HATTON

+ 600m ALTITUDE

STONE RETAINING WALLS

BUNKHOUSE

← ROAD

TERRACES (ALMOND GROVES)

300m

TERRACES (ALMOND GROVES)

TERRACES (ALMOND GROVES)

TERRACES (ALMOND GROVES)

DISTANCE TO VALLDEMOSA 7.5m

SOBs
RED HAMMER DOWN

JACK HILD

A GOLD EAGLE BOOK FROM
WORLDWIDE

TORONTO · NEW YORK · LONDON · PARIS
AMSTERDAM · STOCKHOLM · HAMBURG
ATHENS · MILAN · TOKYO · SYDNEY

First edition May 1985

ISBN 0-373-61606-6

Special thanks and acknowledgment to
Alan Philipson for his contributions to this work.

Printed in Canada

1

William Starfoot II's captors were extremely prudent men. They had taken great pains to immobilize all six-foot-six inches of him on the hospital bed. His right leg was encased from toes to crotch in a heavy plaster cast. He lay flat on his back, securely strapped to the mattress by thick leather belts running from the metal bedframe over ankles, knees, hips, chest, chin and forehead. They could not strap down Billy Two's lips. He sucked in a breath as deep as the restraints would allow and addressed the semicircle of lab-coated, clipboard-wielding tormentors. What burst from his throat was not the scathing string of obscenity and personal insult he had intended, but unintelligible croaking, abruptly terminated. Even to Billy Two it sounded inhuman, a chicken's final squawk as its neck was wrung. The assembled psychiatrists and medical technicians conferred in Russian, nodding as though pleased with the content and character of the outburst.

Tears of frustration rolled down Billy's cheeks. Not only was the half-Navaho, half-

Osage unable to communicate, he couldn't even work up a decent rage over the failure: the effect of stupid juice, the pink fluid they injected into his forearms six times daily. It had turned Billy Two's tongue into a huge, numbed thing glued to the roof of his mouth by spittle thick as library paste. His mind was likewise numbed. To raise a thought from the morass of consciousness was to fight against the unrelenting force of gravity.

And to fight was to pay.

Blackness swept across his field of vision from left to right, a rushing wall of riveted iron plate. In its wake there was another hallucination, an auditory one: a chilling whine with Doppler effect, as if something enormous had hurtled by him at tremendous speed. For a second the world spun madly, and he was sure he was going to pass out. Then the tiny seizure was over. It left Billy Two with a lingering metallic taste in his mouth, aware of his tear-streaked cheeks but unable to remember why he was crying.

One of the uniformed men bent over him and spoke. He had a full beard, mousy brown shot with white, and no hair at all on his head. The words in English filtered down to Starfoot as if slowed to half speed, the voice an artificial baritone.

"Because you have been so violent and uncooperative," the psychiatrist said, "we have arranged for an addition to your treatment and regimen.''

Violent and uncooperative.

Billy Two managed an idiotic smile. He didn't recall being either. But he hoped to bloody hell he had.

The bearded man turned to a technician who held a white enameled tray. From the tray, the psychiatrist took a hypodermic syringe and a small glass bottle. He inserted the tip of the needle into the bottle's rubber protective membrane and filled the syringe with a clear liquid. ''This is sulfazine,'' the man told Billy. ''A mixture of one percent sterile sulfur in peach-kernel oil. It is standard therapeutic medication for difficult patients such as you. We are confident it will have the desired effect.''

He squirted a little of the fluid onto the tray to clear air bubbles from the syringe, then plunged the needle into Billy's arm.

The stuff burned going in.

''Oh, fuck,'' the Indian groaned.

It kept on burning. A brushfire crept straight up his arm, shoulder, neck. Nerves along the path of the sulfazine went berserk; his right hand became a trembling claw on the starched sheet as biceps sinew and ligament went suddenly rigid and shoulder-group muscles twitched in a frenzy. Then the shit hit his head.

Billy Two screamed, his back arching against the mattress, making the heavy, black strap cut deep into the flesh of his chest. Sulfur fire exploded inside his skull, a breaking wave of fever heat so intense that it sent sweat jetting from every pore. He could feel the spongy mass of his brain sizzling, crisping; his eyeballs melting, oozing like raw egg whites from between his clenched eyelids.

Then his abdominal muscles convulsed. His abdomen turned into a washboard with a mind and purpose all its own, hellbent on rearing up, tearing itself free of his torso. If he had been able to draw himself into a fetal ball, the cramps might have been bearable, but the restraining straps held him stretched out flat, strung taut and quivering.

The Indian prayed for the black iron wall to zoom past, for the taste of metal, for the sweet, utter obliteration of his agony. No well came. The sulfur drug was too powerful; it overwhelmed and canceled the effects of the stupid juice.

The convulsion gradually eased, and Billy Two slumped back to the bed. His gray cotton gown was sopping wet, his pulse pounding, the lining of his throat and nose scorched, seared with every intake of breath. As a side effect of the convulsive shock, his mind seemed clearer than it had been in weeks. Through a waving veil of flame he viewed the stark mental-hospital room. There were no shades or bars on the bulletproof windows; they were painted white halfway up to prevent the inmates from seeing the Moscow street beyond, to prevent the urbanites strolling along Smolensk Boulevard from glimpsing the tormented creatures who dwelt within.

He viewed the room's occupants as well. The pale fish-belly faces hidden behind beards, mustaches, shaggy sixties-era muttonchop sideburns. Only five of them, he thought. Five weak little men with soft throats just beyond his reach when he wanted so much to tear their pasty necks apart, to bloody his arms to the elbows in brutal and permanent disassembly of trachea, esophagus, larynx.

His fingers raked the sheets as the stomach cramps returned with a vengeance, this time determined to double him up despite the rows of straps. The agonizing pressure in his gut swelled while he held his breath, every muscle straining against the sustained contraction. His heart thudded crazily, its beats jammed end to end, indistinguishable, until they formed a terrifying droning in his chest. He felt a cold, ripping sensation under his breastbone and heavy liquid gushing into his chest, filling his lungs. The smell and taste of blood rushed up from his windpipe to his mouth and nose.

Then things happened in a mad rush.

Very curious things.

The Indian did not black out. He slipped out. His consciousness expelled, whole and aware, from the shuddering body by a kind of psychic peristalsis. Formless, he floated to the ceiling and stopped, resting there like a helium-filled balloon. He looked down on the body strapped to the bed, a rigid body, quaking violently, mouth gaping, teeth bared, eyes bulging. The mass of bone and muscle below him was in horrible pain but Billy Two experienced it only indirectly, in a sympathetic way; he was a spectator at his own chemical crucifixion.

A terrible realization struck Starfoot from his disembodied vantage. What had just happened to him was exactly what all the supermarket tabloids claimed death was like in countless cover stories about people clinically dead who had come back to life. The out-of-body experience. Oh, shit, am I already dead? he thought.

"No, you're not dead," a strange voice assured him.

It was not speech, really. He did not hear the words so much as read them in his mind.

Billy looked around the room for the source of the remark. Where there had been five men, there were now six. And the newcomer was not a staff member of the infamous Serbsky Institute. He was as tall and brown as Billy Two, naked except for a beaded buckskin loincloth. He wore an intricately crafted mask that covered his entire head. Human eyes, black, shiny and cold as stream-washed stones, stared out of the feathered, razor-beaked face of a bird of prey. Plumed raptor wings were strapped to the creature's arms and shoulders. The psychiatrists were not alarmed by his presence; in fact, they didn't seem to notice him at all.

If I'm not dead, I've lost it. All those fucking drugs. They finally did the job on my head, Billy told himself.

"Do you know know what I am?" the hawk-man asked.

"Symbol of my father's tribe, the Osage," Billy Two replied.

"Spirit," the intruder corrected. "That which cannot be broken. Cannot be altered."

Billy Two did not argue. He accepted his fellow phantasm without question. The presence of Hawk Spirit, conjured out of drug or pain overdose or a combination of both, deeply soothed and comforted him.

"Why the hell are they doing this to me?" Billy asked. "I can't remember anything. What do they want from me?"

"They are tormenting you because you as a warrior have hurt them badly, have caused them to lose valued men and much face. Because you had the poor luck to fall wounded into their hands. The only purpose to your pain is to give them the pleasure of vengeance."

"Will I die?"

"Every man dies."

Hawk Spirit was something of a tease. "Will I

die down there, on the bed?'' Billy snapped back.

"Part of you has already died."

"They've disfigured me?"

The spirit said nothing.

Billy Two gazed down at his physical body trembling against the restraints. "I see no wound."

"Inside," the spirit said, stepping through the solid forms of the Russian psychiatrists as if they were made of mist, pointing a soft wingtip at the left temple of Billy Two's perspiration-drenched head. "Inside here."

"Am I a vegetable?"

Behind the feather-rimmed eye sockets of the hawk mask, obsidian eyes glittered. "You are an Osage. Tall. Straight. Strong. There is nothing these pale scurrying creatures can do to change that."

"But you're telling me I'm brain-damaged!"

"Wounds heal. And sometimes the wounded one comes out stronger than before."

"Will I do that?"

"Your future is in your hands."

"Will you show me how to heal?"

"I will, but to succeed you must endure much suffering. You must return to the bed."

"Have I choice?"

"Yes," Hawk Spirit said, "you can die. Without further pain."

"Like a bug on a pin?"

There was no reply.

Billy Two stared down at his own tortured, sweat-soaked form. He did not think about the excruciating agony he had just fled. He thought about his father, William Starfoot I, a full-blooded Osage, who for the previous forty years had been content to sit on his ass in his immense Oklahoma mansion fondling his oil shares, figuring his profits, watching his fortunes grow.

Assimilated. Co-opted. Bought out.

And William Starfoot I had done all he could, short of disinheriting his only son, to get him to fall in line, to give up the booze and the bimbos, and the terrible hazards and hardships of the mercenary life. None of the enticements had worked.

If paternal gifts of love did not have the power to mellow him, a threat of pain dispensed by hated strangers had no chance whatsoever.

"I'll pay the price to live on, Hawk Spirit," Billy Two said. "To live on and kick ass."

As he started to drift down from the ceiling, the door to the room opened and another man entered. No doctor, he was dressed in a well-tailored VDV (Airborne Forces) captain's uniform. Black-haired, tall, athletically built, his handsome, vaguely Asian face was marred by a tightness, a brittleness around the eyes—the look of a man recently wounded and too soon on his feet. As the psychiatrists turned toward him, the officer gestured at the convulsing body on the bed and cracked a joke in Russian.

A very funny joke, apparently.

It put the Serbsky Institute staff in stitches. One of the orderlies was so tickled he lost his grip on the tray he held. It clattered to the linoleum floor, its glass syringe and medicine vial shattering into tiny bits. The staff continued to laugh until tears streamed down their faces.

It was to their braying accompaniment that Billy Two returned to the burning body on the bed.

CAPTAIN BALANDIN WATCHED with pleasure as the Ministry of Health psychiatrists and their flunkies shook with laughter.

The joke, a droll comment on how much improved their patient looked, hadn't been all that funny.

That, in fact, was the real joke.

There were many special benefits available to Balandin as an officer of Spetsnaz, the Soviet Union's most elite and secret combat force: excellent pay, a spacious apartment, a car, state-subsidized international travel, veritable carte blanche on prohibited black-market items. Yet sometimes he was certain that the most wonderful perk of all was nothing tangible. Sometimes he was sure it was simply the power to make groveling asses of supposedly superior men, men of distinguished education with professional credentials, prestige and an inordinate pride in their own accomplishments.

The power he held was, of course, the power of fear. On the most obvious level it was a function of his physical size and consummate martial skills; it was the harm he, personally and in short order, could dispense. But there was also the damage he could indirectly bring about, through surrogates in the massive tangle of Soviet bureaucracy. Damage in the long term. Damage unto the sons and daughters of the sons and daughters.

"Such wit!" the bearded doctor exclaimed, shaking his head, wiping his eyes with a handkerchief.

"Wonderful!" added his colleague with the bushy sideburns.

One of the orderlies repeated the remark over and over to himself, as if memorizing it for later retelling, chuckling as he did so.

"And how are we feeling, today, Captain?" the bearded psychiatrist asked with professional solicitude.

Balandin's mood did an abrupt 180—from mild amusement to nearly homicidal rage. He did not like being reminded of his recent infirmity or any of the problems relating to it. When he wasn't thinking about what had been done to him, when he was in uniform on official Spetsnaz business, he could feel that his testicles were still there, as if the grisly injury had never happened, as if it had all been a terrible dream. A reminder of the event, no matter how slight, started a tape loop of distilled fury, a product of his convalescence, weeks of reliving, rewriting the incident. He could see the beautiful face of the American woman doctor, Leona Hatton; he could feel his own burning desire as he advanced on her, penis in one hand, commando knife in the other. She was irresistible to him, the kind of proud, defiant woman he most enjoyed brutalizing and raping, the kind he invariably stabbed to death at climax. As he got close to her, about to put the blade to her neck, her hands moved so quickly he felt nothing—until she snapped back her right fist. Pain and realization hit at the same instant. As the impossible hurt slammed him to his knees, he saw his bulging scrotum clutched tightly in her fingers, no longer a part of him, glistening vascular vermicelli trailing all down her forearm. He fantasized that, despite the agony and shock of a manual castration, he had grabbed her, pulled her down and strangled her. The truth was considerably less impressive: he had fainted dead away. One week later, as he slipped into his jacket, about to leave the hospital, he had fainted again. Upon sticking his hand in a side pocket he had discovered a present the American had left for him: his missing testicles.

Balandin indicated the brown man in the bed with a jerk of his thumb. "Can this one travel?"

The doctors couldn't hide their disappointment. There would be no more pharmacological fun and games with the helpless American. "Technically, yes," the bearded one said. "He has recovered remarkably well from the thigh wound he received. His mental state, however, is confused and irrational. We believe the patient should be kept in maximum restraint and under sedation at all times. In our opinion he has the potential for outbursts of psychotic violence."

Balandin glared at the psychiatrist. He didn't need to be told how dangerous the Indian was. The man in the bed, along with the bitch Hatton and a handful of other American mercenaries, had done permanent injury to more than just the captain's family tree. Professional hooligans and murderers, known as the Soldiers of Barrabas, had embarrassed and humiliated not only Spetsnaz but its parent organization, GRU, Soviet Military Intelligence, with a grandiose and suicidal scheme to free a famous dissident from a Siberian gulag. A scheme that could never have worked without the tacit consent of KGB—GRU's arch-bureaucratic rival.

The damage to the reputation of GRU was almost incalculable. It could only be compared to the scandals of 1958 and 1962 when it was discovered that high-ranking GRU officers were double agents for CIA and M.I.6. KGB took these events as licence to engage in what it called "prophylaxis," exposing and nipping "further" crimes in the bud. This included arrests of upper-echelon GRU personnel and their replacement with bona fide KGB men. Some of the military intelligence officers, rather than subjecting themselves and their families to painful and all-too-familiar penal and ostracism procedures, had chosen to take their own lives. Among them was Balandin's longtime mentor and father figure, Major Yevgeny Grabischenko. That Balandin had escaped the righteous wrath of KGB was only due to the severity and intimate nature of his injury.

"Get him ready, then," the captain said. "I will send a car around this evening."

The psychiatrists exchanged uncomfortable looks.

"His medication," the bearded one said. "You must maintain the dosage or he will become uncontrollable."

"My people know how to give an injection. Make sure we are provided with enough sedative to last five days."

"Aminazine for only five days?" the psychiatrist said. "You will be bringing him back to Serbsky, then?"

Balandin smiled. The unwritten rule of thumb was never give an explanation when no explanation was required.

"Ready by eight," he said, turning on his heel, exiting the room. He advanced down the dead-white corridor in long, easy strides. He would not be bringing the brown man back.

2

Alex "the Greek" Nanos exhaled through gritted teeth as he swung the chromed curl bar up for the twenty-fifth time, applying the full power of both arms. In the reflection of the weight room's wall of mirrors, he watched the progress of the bar, concentrating on keeping it perfectly level. The center of the bar came even with his chin, his tanned face twisting into a grimace of maximum effort, sweat sliding down from his dark, curly hair over his forehead and cheeks. The biceps and traps exposed by his gray tank top bulged alarmingly, soda-straw veins standing out on the engorged slabs of muscle.

Cooked. His arms felt like so much well-done roast beef as he lowered the bar, but he tried for one more rep at 135 pounds. He got the bar halfway up before he started to come apart, before upper torso became Twitch City. Despite the support of the wide leather kidney belt he wore, the muscles at the sides of his waist began to lock and cramp up.

The only way he could lift the bar to his chin was to cheat—to use the considerable momentum of the bar and the strength of his back and legs. In weight training, a noncompetitive sport, cheating was something you did only to yourself. Muttering a curse, he let the bar down slowly and slid it back onto its iron cradle. Then he picked up a towel and mopped his face and shoulders.

"You really hate that bar, don't you?" said a husky feminine voice behind him.

Nanos stared in the mirror, his expression decidedly hostile. He did not like distractions when he was lifting. He made a habit of visiting the health club at the slowest time of day, when the soap operas were on TV, to ensure he'd have the weight room all to himself.

She was blond, no more than twenty-five, dressed in a lavender exercise leotard so radically French cut he could see bare skin two inches above her hipbones.

The Greek's intimidating look softened at once.

The leotard made long legs appear to be even longer. Powerful legs they were, too. The lady was a serious bodybuilder; she wore fingerless, white leather gloves to keep her palms from callusing. Her arms were so lean and perfectly developed they were like a drawing out of Gray's *Anatomy*. If her skin hadn't been such a deep golden tan, her lack of overall body fat would have been off-putting. Under the front of the tight-fitting leotard her abdomen was a gridwork of interlocking blocks. Her breasts, though small, retained a rounded, thoroughly feminine shape. But they looked solid, not soft, because of the extraordinary pectoral development beneath.

"I guess I should explain," she told him. Under the fringe of bangs, there was a playful twinkle in her steady brown eyes. "I've been watching you work out for a couple of weeks now. Sneaking a peek off and on when you weren't looking. I don't think I've ever seen anybody hit the weights harder than you do. It's like you're trying to kill them before they kill you. Are you training for competition or just burning off the world's biggest mad?"

Nanos slung his towel over his shoulder. Smart lady, he thought. Smart, sexy lady. He was burning off a mad, all right, a mad at himself. And grief. Grief on an order of magnitude he had never felt before. Four weeks back he had lost the best and truest friend he had ever had.

William Starfoot II had bought the farm in Siberia.

And Alex Nanos had had to hear about it secondhand. About how the SOBs couldn't recover the body because of heavy and deadly accurate Russian machine-gun fire. If he'd been allowed on the Soviet penetration leg of the mission, instead of being sent to Rio to handle the hardware details of the complicated bait-and-switch scheme they had pulled on GRU, he would've brought Billy Two back alive—or damn well have died trying.

Billy Two and Alex Nanos had been a team, running buddies, long before they joined up with Nile Barrabas and his SOBs. They had first met in an East Oakland bar on the day of their discharges from service in Nam—Billy from the Marines, the Greek from the Coast Guard. Over a couple of dozen tequila shooters apiece, they had discovered many common interests. They both drank to excess as a matter of principle; they both chased pretty women as if the end of the world was fifteen minutes away; and, above all, they both dearly loved to get into trouble . . . just to see what would happen. And, as it turned out, the two of them together managed to get into ten times the scrapes they had on their own.

For Nanos, the loss of his friend was like the loss of some vital organ from his body; with the Indian gone, life did not taste nearly so sweet. Weight lifting had become the ultimate self-flogging ritual. Bench presses and mea culpas. As a result of the concentrated, obsessive effort, he was stronger, leaner, harder than he'd been in more than ten years.

"Anything worth doing is worth doing one hundred percent," he told the blonde.

"You don't like the meat market much, do you?" she said. "That's why I never see you here early in the morning or after six."

The Greek smiled. He didn't like Los Pavos Health Club and Spa much, period. For one thing it didn't smell like any of the gyms he had ever hung out in before. It was too goddamn clean. Like an airport. Or a Vegas hotel. No soul. In Southern California fitness was big business. Gyms had replaced discos as the number-one places to score with members of the opposite, or the same, sex. It was the I'm-healthy-you're-healthy scene.

That meant designer sweat suits. Designer jockstraps. Designer athlete's foot.

Things Nanos could easily live without. The trouble was, he had no choice. There was the only one gym in town; the town being Los Pavos, a bedroom beach community serving both Los Angeles and Orange County. It served Alex Nanos as a neat little hidey-hole, a place where he could disappear until all the furor over the freeing of the Soviet dissident Leonov blew away. If it ever did.

"You have such sad, sleepy eyes," the woman remarked. "Bedroom eyes. I bet you've been told that before."

"No, never," he lied. They *all* said that. From Acapulco to Biarritz. Funny thing, though, the Greek never got tired of hearing it.

"How do you feel about saunas?" the blonde asked.

"Why?"

She put her hand lightly on his bare shoulder.

Again there was that twinkle in her level gaze. "Because I just love 'em. And this time of day there's never anybody in the one they've got here."

Nanos got the picture. For almost a month he had gone without female companionship. That had been part of his self-inflicted punishment. Alone in his marina condo he had thought he'd missed women, longed for women, but those yearnings were nothing compared to the yen he felt now.

The blonde drew her fingernails gently but firmly down the length of his arm, all the way to his palm. "Well, what do you say? Shall we?"

If she hadn't been so damn good-looking and so damned eager, Nanos might have held out. Might have, though the odds were better than ten to one against. The Greek's successful abstinence was a function of forced isolation, not willpower. The wheels of rationalization started grinding at once, his resolve crumbling as the fingernail-induced chills rippled up his backbone. Billy Two hadn't asked him to go celibate as a penance; that had been his own dumb idea. If Billy could see him now, even considering not doing it to her, he would laugh his head off.

"Lead the way," he said through a broad grin.

She marched ahead of him, giving him ample opportunity to study the wonders of her posterior, the precision fit of muscular buttocks as they slid against each other. Nanos and the blonde walked in time to the FM rock music oozing perpetually from the PA system, past the health club's tiled lobby, the indoor fountain splashing amid artfully placed rubber trees, the natural-juice bar, which also served beer from around the world, the exhibition racquetball courts with back walls of glass. The only person they saw was the guy behind the reception desk. He didn't look up from his book as they passed by.

The sauna was right off the Olympic-size indoor pool and Jacuzzi, a cedar-lined room with a sliding glass door opening onto the pool deck.

As the blonde pushed the door back, she glanced over her shoulder at him, an expression of concern on her pretty face. "Say, you're not getting cold feet, are you?" she asked. "Afraid someone will see us at it?"

Nanos laughed out loud. The possibility of drawing an audience hadn't even occurred to him, though obviously anyone entering the pool room could see straight into the sauna. "Hey, if they can't take a joke . . ." he said, stepping into the stiflingly hot cubicle behind her and sliding the door shut.

She kicked off her aerobicize shoes and without a word started peeling out of her leotard.

Oh, my, Nanos thought as she slid the garment down her legs, then stepped out of it. She was tan all over. Except for the pale pink tips of her breasts. Below the line of her lavender terry-cloth headband, which she did not bother to remove, tiny beads of perspiration had already begun to trickle down the sides of her face. Her arms, her breasts, her belly glistened.

"Well?" she said, putting a still protectively gloved hand on her cocked hip.

Nanos nearly did himself an injury stripping out of his gym shorts. When he was naked, she slipped into his arms, her taut nipples grazing, tickling his chest, her slick belly trapping his already upraised member between them. They kissed for a long moment, open mouthed, greedy tongues exploring, then she pushed back, out of breath.

"You sit," she told him, "I'll ride."

The Greek sat on the hot wooden bench, leaning back against the wall. Sweat poured off him in a steady stream as she straddled his lap, kneeling on the edge of the bench. He ran his hands down her sides and cupped her smooth, rounded bottom.

Further foreplay was forgone.

With simultaneous and well-coordinated hand and hip movement, she guided him into her.

"Holy shit," Nanos groaned softly as the blonde set about impaling herself in a near frenzy, the powerful muscles of her stomach and pelvis doing amazing things to him.

Too amazing.

Think about something else! he told himself, biting the tip of his tongue, driving back the onrushing wave of pleasure with sharp pain.

The blonde raised her arms overhead, stretching, writhing on his lap like a wounded snake. Then her fingers touched the side of her headband as if she was about to take it off. Something bright and impossibly thin, a spiderweb of silver, slithered out from under the terry cloth and snapped taut between her gloved hands.

The strand of stainless steel was around the Greek's neck before he could get his hands up. It was twisted tight, slicing into the skin of his throat like a razor, cutting off his air. The blonde locked the garrote over his Adam's apple with a series of frantic overhand cross turns.

"Die, bastard!" she cried into his purpling face, grabbing his wrists, fighting to keep his hands away from his neck, her hips, if anything, churning faster, wilder than before.

Nanos only played patty-cake with her for a moment. Long enough to realize she had both the strength and the skill to keep him in the wire noose for another sixty seconds.

His last sixty seconds.

The Greek lunged forward, bashing his forehead against her nose. It gave with a sickening crunch. She did not. As Nanos reared back for another head butt, he saw blood spurt from her nostrils, down over her mouth, chin and chest.

It did not dim the gleam in her eyes or slow her mad gyrations on his lap.

Nanos hit her with everything he had. The solid impact of skull on skull stunned him. For a second everything went black, then he felt her hands slip from his wrists, her suddenly limp body falling back, sliding down between his parted legs. She dropped to the floor in a heap.

His lungs screaming, his vision tunneling out, Alex struggled with the turns of wire. He untwisted the garrote and gasped for breath, prying the strand of wire from its gory burrow in his flesh.

The PA system started blaring a Rolling Stones oldie as the blonde scrambled to her feet. Shrieking at him in Russian, her face a bloody ruin, she fired a roundhouse kick to his head.

It glanced off his cheek, but the snap of impact sent the back of his skull slamming into the sauna wall. She was playing to win. Nanos ducked under a second kick and came off the bench in a shallow dive. His shoulder hit her single supporting leg below the knee and she went flying over his back, crashing into the bench and the wall. He was on her before she could recover, grabbing her by the hair and the back of the neck. He swung her around like a rag doll, ramming the top of her head against the inside of the heavy plate-glass door.

It made a hollow, thudding sound; she made no sound at all. The pane quivered but did not shatter.

He dragged her back and rammed again.

And again.

And again.

Until the armored glass finally cracked, spider-shattering away from the great pink smear he had made of cranium and contents.

Nanos slumped back to the bench seat and mopped his face with his towel. Then he tried to wipe his hands on it; they were shaking uncontrollably.

From the PA speaker outside the sauna, Mick Jagger sang as if to him: "You can't always get what you wa-ant."

Nanos regarded the dead woman at his feet.

"No shit, Sherlock."

3

Liam O'Toole gestured at his collected works, the loose pile of yellowed, dog-eared manuscript on the New York agent's littered desk and asked, "So, what did you think of my stuff?"

Clive Walloon, jackal among the lions of literature, pale, chinless, thoroughly cloaked in English tweeds down to his boxer shorts, smiled winningly at the unpublished poet and said, "Have you ever thought about greeting cards?"

"Have I ever thought *what* about greeting cards?"

Walloon's smile broadened. The bigger it got, the phonier it looked. "Have you ever considered writing verse for greeting cards?"

"You mean like 'Happy Birthday' and 'Get Well Soon'?"

"There's a nice dollar in it."

"Did you read my poems?" the red-haired man asked incredulously.

"I looked through them. I think you have the fundamentals of the craft down pretty well. I think you're ready to make the big move up into the professional ranks. All you need is a little direction. Some confidence."

"My poems are about war."

"And they show real imagination."

"I didn't make them up out of the air," O'Toole told him. "They're based on things that actually happened, to me or to my buddies."

Walloon gave him a doubtful look.

"I want to get those poems in print," Liam told him, pointing at the pile amid the other piles, the pile that was his.

The agent stared up at the ceiling and slowly shook his head. So exasperated, so put upon, so patronizing, as he finally deigned to explain the facts of life to the stocky man seated across from him. "Those poems are not commercial. Believe me, I know what I'm talking about. They're too personal and obsessive. Too overboard with the graphic violence. Too juvenile in philosophy. The only way you're going to get that stuff in print is to pay somebody out of your own pocket to publish it. We call it 'vanity' or 'self' publishing."

Liam took his own poetry very seriously, even if nobody else did. He took criticism seriously, too. Especially negative criticism. At that moment he wanted nothing more than to feed the agent his own Harris tweed sport jacket, sleeves first.

"Look, my friend," Walloon said, "it's time for you to move on, to expand your horizons, stretch your skills."

"By writing Mother's Day cards? Hey, I'm a serious poet."

"I realize that. That's why I'm suggesting you get yourself into a professional situation. There's nothing like working under deadline pressure to bring out the best in a writer. It's what separates the men from the boys."

"Or the hacks from the artists."

Walloon glanced meaningfully at his gold Rolex. A busy and important man such as he didn't have time to waste arguing with nobodies. "I can't do anything with your first submission to me. All the horror comics went out of business twenty-five years ago. Nobody else is going to buy your war poems. If you want to apply yourself, do your homework, study what's in the marketplace, put in some time working out samples of verse for different occasions, I'll be glad to take your portfolio around to the card people. I think you stand a good chance of getting in at one of the major companies. A very good chance."

"Assuming I do what you suggest and they want me, what's your cut going to be?"

"The standard rate. Twenty percent of everything you make."

O'Toole rose slowly from his seat. He reached across the desk and picked up his poems. His "juvenile" poems. He paused and then put the manuscript back on the desk. Then he reached across the desk a second time and picked up Clive Walloon, lifting him one-handed from a sitting to a standing position by his knit tie. The admittedly juvenile urge to do violence to Clive-baby and to the carefully selected furnishings of his Manhattan office was almost more than O'Toole could control. What made him even madder was the knowledge that breaking the face of a slimeball wimp or trashing his place of business would alter nothing in the grand scheme of things. It would not make Walloon a better agent; it would not get a major house interested in his poetry.

Sometimes, though, a guy had to do a thing because it needed to be done, not because it would change the world.

Liam hauled the agent and his much-stretched tie through the clutter of his desk top, dragging the lower half of the tie over the desk's front edge. From the litter he picked up a stone paperweight and a silver letter opener. As O'Toole raised the four-pound hunk of agate high over Walloon's head, the agent began to squawk: "Fifteen! Dear God, I'll take fifteen!"

Liam used the paperweight like a hammer, pounding the letter opener's point through the tie and deep into the front of the desk. He made a very workmanlike job of it, bending the handle of the opener over like a staple. Then, without uttering another word, Liam picked up his poems, turned and left the office.

He walked down the hall to the elevators. There were cardboard notices taped to both sets of doors. They said the same thing: "Elevator

under repair. We are sorry for the inconve-
nience.''

"Like hell you are," O'Toole uttered, heading for the green-lit Fire Exit sign. He pulled
open the heavy door and started down the dim
stairwell.

He hadn't come to New York City to land a
fucking free-lance job helping to supply the
doggerel needs of the English-speaking world.
He had enough money in the bank to last him
comfortably the rest of his life, thanks to the
six-figure payoffs on his recent missions with
Barrabas. He had come to Manhattan to im-
merse himself in the literary landscape, to
expose himself to the world of big-time publishing, to get himself discovered. If he'd wanted to
publish through one of the vanity houses, he
could have done so in short order. But he
wanted more than just his words pressed into
paper, his name in gold leaf on the calfskin-
grained brown vinyl of a book spine. He wanted
someone else to publish him, someone else to
tell him his work was worthy of seeing print.
The longer he spent trying to become a real
poet, the more it seemed to him that there was
much more dignity in remaining forever un-
sullied, uncompromised, unpublished. He
rolled the wad of yellowed papers and jammed
it in his belt.

O'Toole was halfway down a flight of stairs
when he heard the sound of footsteps from

above. Somebody else was taking the hard way down. As he turned the corner he saw two guys leaning against the wall on the landing directly below him. Two big white guys in heavily soiled overcoats and tennis shoes, with haircuts short enough to pass for either punk-chic or regulation penitentiary. They looked up at him with deadpan faces, hands thrust deep in their overcoat pockets.

The red-haired man stopped right where he was, pausing to evaluate the situation. Were the hidden grubby fingers of his fellow New Yorkers wrapped around their American Express cards or their flick knives? Saturday night specials? Short lengths of galvanized pipe?

The footsteps from above got louder, faster. O'Toole looked over his shoulder in time to see a third man, a clone of the first two, skid to a halt on the steps behind him. Immediately the third guy shoved a hand into his overcoat's slash pocket.

The men below started to inch their way up the staircase, shoulder to shoulder.

"I'll be perfectly honest with you guys," Liam said, dividing his attention equally between the upper and lower sets of punks, "I've had a hell of a piss-poor day and I'm really not in the mood to get mugged. I think you should find yourself another sucker."

The men below stopped. The one on O'Toole's left with newspapers for socks was definitely the boss. The other guy glanced at him for the go-ahead signal. It wasn't a nervous glance, either, the kind of jittery, frazzled look to be expected from a standard-issue urban junkie in way over his head; that is, trying to pull a stairway rip-off with odds of only three to one. It was a look without emotion. Professional.

"But you're just the sucker we're after," the head dirtball told Liam. His right hand came out of his overcoat pocket. In it was a silencer-equipped Makarov 9mm auto. No junkie's gun, for sure.

O'Toole recognized the signature weapon at once. Soviet special forces. He had known he was taking a calculated risk in not going underground after the mission into Siberia with the SOBs. He had figured that, given his highly visible role in the Leonov affair, the Spetsnaz vendetta squads would find him eventually no matter where he ran to.

Running from trouble wasn't one of Liam O'Toole's strong points, anyway.

"Is that GRU's new uniform for spring?" he asked them. "I hate to break it to you girls, but I've seen that style all over town."

The head man said something in Russian to his two comrades. Their hands came out of their pockets, too. Not wrapped around the grips of autopistols, but the handles of double-edged, commando daggers. The two Spetsnaz soldiers started closing in on O'Toole while their head man held the Makarov aimed rock-steady at his center chest.

Liam got the picture, but quick. They were trying to make his execution look like a routine Big Apple robbery-murder. Stab wounds did not excite forensic pathologists the way unique Russian-caliber slugs did. They actually expected him to stand there and let them jab him full of holes in preference to a nice clean bullet through the heart.

The red-haired man put his back against the stairwell wall as the pair of assailants moved within striking distance. O'Toole angled himself so the guy coming up the stairs acted as a screen, cutting off the head man's line of fire for a second. If the Spetsnaz leader had been using a gun chambered for 9mm parabellum, instead of the less powerful 9x18mm Makarov round, the torso of his comrade wouldn't have served as a barrier for Liam to hide behind. The slugs would have gone right through. As it was, the leader had to shift his position on the landing below to keep his target covered.

O'Toole didn't give him time to line things up.

He squatted and lunged right, throwing an arm behind the heels of the killer above. With a single powerful sweep he ripped the guy's legs out from under him. The Spetsnaz soldier crashed to his back on the steel-capped edges of the steps. Liam didn't tear the dagger from the man's hand; he turned both hand and dagger, unresisting in the moment of shock, and with the full weight of his body drove the blade under the man's breastbone to the hilt. O'Toole rolled away as the soldier gasped and stiffened, clutching at the dagger handle, continuing to slide thrashing, kicking down the steps.

The way above was now clear, but O'Toole couldn't take it. Not unless he wanted a bullet in the spine. The trooper below him feinted and jabbed at his face. Liam kept the man between him and the Makarov. Unfortunately that meant staying nose to nose with him.

The leader shouted at his man, trying to get him out of the way so he could take a killing shot. O'Toole read the eyes of the knife-waving soldier. He wanted to do the job, himself. Liam dodged a dagger thrust to the groin, then snap-kicked. The point of impact, the soldier's chin, jerked straight up from the force of the kick. O'Toole hopped down two steps and drove his meaty forearm into the soft spot at the base of the man's exposed throat. It was a solid hit. A bona fide larynx-crusher. The soldier's face went white, then red, then magenta; his mouth opened to scream, but all that came out was a terrible shrill whistle.

O'Toole grabbed him around the waist. The human shield shuddered against Liam as the silenced Makarov began to cough. Zip, thwack! Zip, thwack! The 9mm slugs burrowed into the dying soldier's back. The autopistol held eight rounds, way too many to dodge. O'Toole heaved the trembling body away from him, sending it flying backward down the stairs and onto the leader below. He threw himself after it.

The leader reeled back, twisting out from under the dead weight of his own man. Before he could get the pistol on track again, he had Liam in his face.

O'Toole got control of the man's gun hand, putting his shoulder into the guy's chest, turning him, smashing the edge of his wrist over the stairway railing. On the fourth smash the leader let go of the gun. It fell, clattering to the lower floors.

He drove himself into Liam's back, trying to knock him over the railing as well. His left forearm slid across the front of O'Toole's throat, cutting off his air.

Liam locked his left hand around the man's left wrist and pulled outward and down, a reverse curl. It was a contest for a few seconds, both men straining for control, then the American got just enough slack to slip the choke hold. He twisted away to the left but he didn't let go of the Russian's wrist. He held it tight and punched with his right fist. Punched cross chest into the side of the much taller man's head. Knuckles rapped hard against unprotected temple.

Stunned, the leader staggered, his eyes momentarily sightless, and then the two of them stumbled together down to the lower landing. As they did so, the Russian got a solid grip on

O'Toole's left wrist as well. Then they both started swinging for all they were worth.

It was like a dance.

The pair of them locked wrist to wrist, turning round and round, trading full-power right-hand shots to the head. It was definitely O'Toole's kind of contest. Grinning through bloodied teeth and nose, he poured it on the Russian. Overhand after overhand, the blows rattled his arm all the way to the shoulder. The return blows got weaker and fewer; in short order, he was throwing five to one. Then the Russian's legs faltered, knees buckling, and he dropped to his butt on the landing.

Liam stepped over and behind him, bending down, taking hold of gory chin in one hand and opposing shoulder in the other. With a precise application of force, he snapped the semiconscious man's neck.

O'Toole let the soldier slump forward onto his face. Then he straightened up, massaging his battered jaw as he surveyed the grotesquely sprawled bodies. He had been lucky. Goddamn lucky. He pushed away from the wall and trotted down the stairs as fast as his wobbly legs would go. He had to get the word out to Barrabas and the others.

Spetsnaz was on the hunt.

4

Captain Balandin strutted down the line of rigidly erect, uniformed men and women, his keen eyes measuring each one. They stood at full attention in the wind-whipped interior courtyard of Moscow's nine-story Khodinsk building, supreme headquarters of GRU. There were fifty-eight of them. Half a company of the motherland's finest, drawn from naval and airborne units stationed all over the Soviet Union, all under the command of Balandin, their lives committed by their superiors to the total destruction of the Soldiers of Barrabas.

"I am satisfied," Balandin told his tall, gaunt-cheeked lieutenant. He squinted up at the leaden, February sky. It was starting to spit sleet. "I want to talk to you and the sergeants before we deploy. Meet me in my office in five minutes."

"The troops, sir?" Lieutenant Skorokhvatov asked.

"Let them stand," Balandin said, turning away and walking into the teeth of the wind. A little cold air and a bit of wet snow would not bother the soldiers of Spetsnaz. Soldiers who went on winter maneuvers without sleeping bags or tents.

Balandin entered the security bunker, a two-story building without windows. He passed the checkpoint, displaying his ID badge to the armed guards who, though they knew him by sight as well as reputation, would not have let him pass without seeing it. Inside the thirty-foot-high perimeter walls of Khodinsk, security was never lax. As he stepped down the hall toward his office, he thought he heard voices behind him, voices and smothered laughter. He stopped and looked back. The guards were facing the other way.

He knew they made fun of him.

They all made fun of him behind his back. He had become a cartoon, a caricature, the self-styled ladies' man who no longer had the wherewithal to take his pleasure.

He even knew what they called him: Ball-less Balandin.

There was nothing he could do about it. To haul someone on the carpet for insubordination was to draw even more unwanted attention to his problem and to his inability to cope with it.

He entered his small office, shut the door and went straight for the hand mirror he kept in his desk's middle drawer. He studied his own face, feeling the stubble on his chin. He had always had a very heavy beard. It had made his skin look blue-dark even after a close shave. As Balandin examined himself, he got a sinking feeling in his gut. He was convinced that his facial hair was getting softer, thinner, day by day. Without testes, he knew he would gradually lose his secondary sex characteristics. The GRU doctors had assured him that with maintenance hormone injections there would be no change in his outward appearance. Despite their repeated assurances, Captain Balandin was terrified, not only of what he would lose—beard, sex drive—but what he would gain.

Soft skin.

Body fat.

Feminine breasts.

A knock on his door startled him out of the self-pitying reverie. He shoved the mirror back in the drawer, slammed it shut, then said, "Enter!"

Skorokhvatov and the three sergeants marched in, saluted and came to attention.

"At ease," Balandin told them, taking a seat behind his desk.

One of the sergeants was a woman. Zoya Ilin. A member of ZSKA, the Soviet Army athletic team. A world-class swimmer, she was a potential Olympic medalist in the 400-meter freestyle event. In her uniform, with her shoulder-length light-brown hair pulled into a tight bun under her cap and her painfully plain face, she might have passed for a man. Balandin scowled at her. There had been rumors that she was taking the same drugs that had been prescribed for him.

"I have had some news from the United States," the captain said. "It is not good. The plainclothes assassination team assigned to eliminate the targets O'Toole and Nanos have failed to complete their missions."

The Spetsnaz sergeants did not blink, nor did their lieutenant.

"We have been told," Balandin continued, "that all of our people are dead. The loss of their lives, though regrettable, will not alter the timetable of our retaliatory strike. We have learned that both of the U.S. targets are in transit to Europe, exactly where we want them. I'm relaying this information to you for one reason only. I want there to be no doubt in your minds about the survival skills of our adversaries. I want you to make sure your troops understand as well."

"We will, sir," Skorokhvatov assured him.

Balandin viewed the row of grim faces. The honor of all had been dirtied by the SOBs, their proud service held up to shame and ridicule in the world press. Inside the Soviet Union access to the truth, the scope of what the mercenaries had done, was tightly controlled, Leonov's escape denied, the sabotage of the Ust Tavda tank plant never mentioned. But the people who counted knew. The members of the ruling politburo. The heads of KGB. Men who could and had put the screws to Spetsnaz from top to bottom.

Sergeant Munshin, a barrel-chested bear of a

man, cleared his throat and said, "Sir? A question, sir."

"Go on."

"What if the SOBs don't cooperate with us? What if they don't band together at their training base on Majorca? What if they scatter instead, all over the Continent?"

"Sergeant, we applied pressure to the targets in the United States and their first reaction was run back to the fold, to join forces with their fellow mercenaries. They know they can't survive alone for long against us. Together, they think they might have a chance. We will herd them like sheep into a place they are confident they can defend and then we will bring the red hammer down, annihilating them to the last man."

Balandin gave Munshin a pained look. "Do you follow my reasoning, Sergeant?"

The burly noncom nodded.

"And you, Khishchuk?" Balandin said, addressing the third sergeant, a massively-built ZSKA shot-putter.

Khishchuk came to attention, his flat, ruddy, moon face devoid of expression. "Yes, sir! Brilliant, sir!"

Balandin turned his gaze on Ilin. He despised all women, but the sudden rush of hatred he felt for the stout dimorphic figure in the VDV uniform was in a separate category. "Have you anything to add?" he asked her.

"No, sir," she said emphatically.

"Then get your troops into plainclothes," Balandin told them.

The lieutenant and sergeants saluted and made a quick and silent exit.

As soon as the door closed, the captain opened the desk drawer and pulled out the hand mirror. For an instant, when he first looked into it, he did not see his own face reflected; he saw instead Sergeant Ilin's. The trick of his mind hit him like a galvanic shock. He shot to his feet, the hair on the back of his neck bristling. Snarling a curse, he hurled the mirror against the far wall.

5

"Aren't they great?" Gunther Dykstra shouted into Nile Barrabas's ear.

The white-haired man winced. He did not like lying to a good friend, so he did not answer. Up on the tiny stage of the Lido, Gunther's Amsterdam nightclub, five long-haired guys in their midforties were singing and playing their hearts out while a psychedelic light show bubbled and swirled over them. The decibel level of the sixties' style rock was ear-splitting, thanks to double drummers beating in unison and an eight-foot-high wall of speakers with driving amplifiers all turned up to ten.

"Haven't changed a bit!" the blond Dutchman bellowed, his face beaming.

Gunther and Barrabas could agree on that point. The nightclub owner, an aficionado of the long-dead San Francisco sound, considered the early work of Crystal Wedge ground-breaking; he saw the reformation of the group with its original members as a milestone in music history. Barrabas saw them exactly as he had at the Fillmore Auditorium in 1966, as a gaggle of supremely untalented geeks. "Yeah!" he shouted back across the tiny, wobbly table. "Their music is just like I remember it."

The lead-guitar player, a guy with a three-foot ponytail of graying hair pulled straight back from midcranium, the current location of his hairline, tiptoed through the chin-high forest of microphone stands to the extreme front edge of the stage and began a solo.

Two bars into it, he broke a string, putting his instrument completely out of tune with itself as well as the accompaniment. He didn't stop to replace it, but kept right on wailing, slashing wild spurts of notes through three keys at a time. And why not? In tune or out of tune, there was no discernible difference in the sounds he made.

"Fan-tastic!" Gunther gushed.

It made Barrabas's teeth stand on edge. He looked around the almost deserted club. Normally, the room was packed on Saturday night with Dutch rockers, punkers and a smattering of international tourists. None of the above wanted any part of Crystal Wedge. But, Gunther wanted them and that was all that mattered. He didn't run the Lido for a profit. It was a hobby that also served as a tax shelter and laundry for his real business: smuggling on a global scale.

The lead guitarist raged on for ten minutes, then after four false endings, finally stopped the band with a downward swing of his guitar and a simultaneous leap in the air. He pulled something in his right leg when he landed, but he was a real trouper. "We love ya!" he shouted into the microphone as the houselights came up, addressing Gunther, Barrabas and the half-dozen others with nerves of steel. Then he limped off the stage.

"What a set," the Dutchman said. "God, I love the way they do 'Bolero.' "

Barrabas shook his head. It was hard to hear over the hiss still echoing in his ears. " 'Bolero'?" he said. "They played 'Bolero'?"

"The last tune."

"Yeah, right."

Gunther gave him a concerned look. "I dragged you down here because I thought these guys would take your mind off Spetsnaz for a little while, at least. You've been stewing over this twenty-four hours a day, seven days a week. You're driving yourself nuts. You're driving me nuts, too."

"They took my mind off Spetsnaz," Barrabas admitted, picking up his glass of Scotch rocks and staring fixedly into its untouched amber depths.

It wasn't like the former U.S. Army colonel to brood over a combat mission once it was completed. As a professional, he had always been able to put the jobs out of his mind, no matter how they had turned out. When he set foot back on safe soil, Barrabas's first impulse was always to find the nearest blonde and the biggest bottle.

To celebrate his continued good health with no thought to the expense or the hangover.

The Siberian mission had been different in a lot of ways. It had succeeded without really succeeding; it had ended without really ending. When the mercenary leader returned to the sanctuary of the Netherlands this time, there was no celebration. No beautiful blonde waiting. He had made sure of that. Before he had left for Russia, Barrabas had sent his longtime lover, Erika, Gunther's sister, to stay with friends in India.

And the booze had lost its kick.

He put the glass down and pushed it aside. The SOBs had managed to rescue the men they had gone in after. It didn't seem to matter to anyone but Barrabas that the famous dissident scientist had been reduced by his Siberian gulag ordeal to little more than a drooling idiot. The men who had financed the expedition, nameless, faceless puppet masters on the world stage, couldn't have been happier with the outcome. They had a living symbol of Soviet inhumanity. A symbol that could not speak for itself, could not complain how it was being used. In the light of what had happened, Barrabas wished he had left Anatoly Leonov where he had found him, sleeping away his last hours peacefully in the snow, his dignity preserved, his remarkable accomplishments left to speak for themselves.

The SOBs had been played for fools on many

levels, by many forces in the gulag rescue. Their success in clearing Soviet airspace with the prize, in slipping past the world's most powerful border defense, had been a gift of KGB, part of its perpetual one-upmanship war with GRU. The loss of the dissident to the West was acceptable to KGB if the entire blame could be laid at the feet of Soviet Military Intelligence.

Barrabas had warned his SOBs before the mission began that if they beat the odds and got out alive, they could expect some kind of organized campaign of retaliation from Spetsnaz. Upon their return to the West, he had paid them off and ordered them all into hiding. Some of the mercenaries had obeyed, in a half-assed way; the rest had chosen to ignore the danger and gone back to their normal lives. Barrabas hadn't ignored the danger, but he had returned to Amsterdam and plain sight. If Spetsnaz couldn't find him, they would go looking for his loved ones.

By far the worst part of the mission for Barrabas had been the loss of William Starfoot II on the gulag airstrip. He was haunted by the memory of the corpse he had been forced to leave behind and the knowledge that a brave fighting man, truly one of a kind, had been sacrificed for nothing.

News of the attempted hits on O'Toole and Nanos had reached him the day before. He had immediately contacted Walker Jessup, liaison between the SOBs and the unofficial—and therefore unaccountable—U.S. government committee that had underwritten recent dirty-tricks missions, including Siberia. Barrabas had asked Jessup, an ex-CIA man who now ran his own independent intelligence network, to arrange for Nanos and O'Toole's secure transport to Amsterdam. What the four of them—Gunther was a prime target, too, having been an indispensable and highly visible part of the Brazilian end of the scam—would do once they linked up was something Barrabas could not decide by himself. In the long term he knew there was no escaping the GRU execution squads; they were too many and too good. If there was a choice involved for him and the others, it was only over where they wanted to stand and fight. A matter for group discussion and democratic process. Barrabas had put a coded ad in the classified section of the *International Herald-Tribune*, warning the other members of the team that Spetsnaz had begun to move.

"Come on, Barrabas," Gunther said, giving his shoulder a firm shake. "Get off your sad-sack butt. There's somebody I want you to meet."

The white-haired man frowned at his old friend. "Not the band, Gunther. Please, not the band."

"Hey, I'll carry you over if I have to."

Barrabas pushed his chair back from the table.

He knew the 260-pound giant would damn well try it, just for a laugh. "You don't have to carry me," he said, standing up.

Gunther waved him on as they filed between the rows of empty tables. The Dutchman made a beeline for the corner of the room nearest the bar. The corner of the room where Crystal Wedge and entourage were taking their well-deserved break.

"Gunther, you are an asshole," Barrabas muttered under his breath.

As the two big men approached, all the red and glassy eyes turned toward them. Hashish smoke hung over the group in a gray cloud.

"This is my friend, Barrabas," the Dutchman said to the band. "He really likes your sound."

If Crystal Wedge hadn't been so fucking pathetic, the white-haired man would have turned and left without a word. He stayed because he was embarrassed for them. They didn't know how bad they were. He stayed and spoke truth, which once past his lips instantly became lies. "I haven't heard a guitar solo like that since '68."

The lead-guitar player switched the hash pipe to his left hand and offered Barrabas his right. "Always glad to meet a fan of the music," he said as they shook hands.

"Right on!" the band members chimed in, raising their clenched fists in the power-to-the-people salute.

Aging, belled and beaded Johnny Appleseeds, the original members of Crystal Wedge were no longer just in it for the bucks. They were on a world pilgrimage. One last road trip to sow the precious seeds of atonal bashing and crashing into yet another generation.

Holy men.

Accompanied by holy women less than half their age.

Gunther ushered one of the latter up to Barrabas. "Saffron," he said, "this is the guy I've been telling you about."

"Far out," said the blond waif in the floor-length, batik-print dress as she sized up the huge man with the white hair. Protruding from under the hem of her skirts were open sandals and tiny bare toes. She had rings on them all. Also a ring through her right nostril.

For years the Dutchman had been threatening to set Barrabas up with one of his wild American "hippie chicks." At last he had made good on the threat. And he was so pleased with himself it was painful to behold.

"I've got some business to take care of up in my office," he said through a vast smirk. "Why don't you two entertain each other for a while?"

"Sounds okay to me," Saffron said, gazing up at Barrabas with big, wondering eyes.

Before the mercenary leader could politely beg off or register a protest, his buddy turned away and took off, leaving them alone.

"What sort of work do you do?" the girl asked, slipping her arm through his and steering him toward a table on the opposite side of the room.

"Free-lance," he said.

"Free-lance what?"

"Lion tamer."

"Come on!"

"I do war work."

He sat down and she sat, too, right on his lap. She stared up at him, searching his face intently for a moment. Then she said, "You have a scary face, Barrabas. But gentle eyes. Do you like war?"

He didn't have to think about the answer to that. "Only an idiot likes war."

"How do you feel about love?" she asked. Without waiting for a reply she threw her slender arms around his neck and kissed him. Her mouth was warm and pliant and her hair smelled of cinnamon.

Barrabas kissed her back. It seemed like the thing to do.

When she finally pulled her mouth away, she looked into his eyes and said, "Is there some place we can go? Some place close?"

"What about your friends in the band? If we leave, they'll have lost a third of their audience."

"The Wedge is used to playing to empty rooms," Saffron told him. "Besides, it builds karma." She touched his cheek with the soft palm of her hand. "Come on," she said, "let's split. You got me in the mood."

Despite intentions to the contrary, Barrabas found himself also very much in the mood. "I know a little hotel two streets over," he said.

She slid off his lap and pulled him to his feet. As they walked for the door, Barrabas waved bye-bye to the boys in the band.

A bit prematurely.

Gunther came barreling down the stairs from his office and cut them off from the exit. "A phone call. You got a phone call, Colonel," he said in a strange, tight voice.

"So, take a message. I'll get back to them later."

Gunther put his arm across the doorway.

"Nile, it's Billy Two."

6

Walker Jessup kept a list in his head.

His asshole list.

On it were the names of the last men in Washington he ever wanted to beg a favor of. Though the lower part of the list changed from time to time, with elections and their corollary—an influx of newer, even bigger buttfaces—the name at the top remained the same.

"The senator is expecting me," Jessup told the statuesque secretary.

She pretended not to notice the 300-pound Texan in the Brooks Brothers tent. She continued typing on her word processor, using two fingers and the time-tested hunt-and-peck method. Her two-and-a-half inch, carmine-painted fingernails made sharp clicking noises on the plastic keys.

Jessup moved around the desk so he could read what she was putting on the CRT. He wasn't surprised to see a computer game, "War of the Zomboids," flickering on the screen. He was surprised to see what a putrid score she had managed to ring up. You'd think, he told himself as he moved closer to her, for a salary of thirty grand a year they could find somebody with the hand-to-eye coordination of a macaque.

He looked over her shoulder, down into the tight creamy chasm, the cleavage of her formidable bosom. A décolletage framed by the plunging neckline of a fuzzy pink cashmere sweater. Underpaid. The poor girl was definitely, criminally underpaid.

"Can I ask you a personal question?" he said.

The senator's secretary kept on tapping the keys. "No," she said without looking away from the screen.

The zomboids were eating her alive no matter how fast she tapped. Or how she held her pouty, full-lipped mouth.

Then the action froze and a buzzer sounded. Endgame.

She turned on her swivel chair to face him. Her eyes narrowed when she saw the focus of his attention, roughly eight inches below the point of her dimpled chin.

"What I want to know is," Jessup continued, "what do you think about when you're with the geezer? When he's got his face squashed in between Mount Everest and K2?"

"Do you have an appointment?"

"Tell him I'm here. He'll give me a minute."

"He left strict orders not to be disturbed this afternoon."

"Wake him. This is important."

She glared at him, but jabbed the intercom button. "Sorry to bother you, Senator, but Mr. Messup is here."

"Funny," the Texan said. "Very amusing."

The senator's disembodied voice erupted from the speaker. "Send him in."

"I know the way," Jessup said, walking past her, heading for the door marked Private. He entered the Capitol Building office and advanced to the front of the massive mahogany desk. The diminutive figure seated on the other side of the oversize piece of furniture looked no different than he had the first time Jessup met him, some ten years before. He was dressed in a black, three-piece suit, black tie, his expression that of a man with chronic constipation. There was a difference, though.

Where once the senator had merely been the world's biggest asshole, he was now the biggest asshole on wheels.

With a nerve-grating whine of electric motor, the senator steered his wheelchair out from behind the desk. "Sit," he told the Texan.

Jessup stood. He stood because he knew it made the senator nervous to have a much bigger man looming over him. The crippled lawmaker might have received the sympathy of a grateful nation, but he got none from Jessup. The fat man knew all. He knew if the senator's constituents ever discovered the real circumstances surrounding his injury, they would strap him to his motorized chair and run it off the nearest pier.

"What do you want?" the legislator demanded.

Jessup took a deep, slow breath before he spoke. "I've been in touch with Barrabas. Two of his SOBs were attacked by Spetsnaz agents within the past twenty-four hours. He believes, and I agree, that GRU is about to repay them for the Siberian raid."

"What has that got to do with me?"

"Since the committee got them into this mess, I think it's the committee's responsibility to get them out. You could arrange for their transport to a military reservation here in the States. A sanctuary that Spetsnaz wouldn't dare violate. They'd only have to stay there long enough to convince the Russians that we are committed to their protection."

"But we aren't," the senator said, making no attempt to conceal his delight.

"What?"

"If the SOBs have a problem, it's theirs, not ours. They were paid to undertake a mission. Very well paid, I might add. They can afford to provide for their own security, I'm sure. You know that the committee wants no connection between the mercenaries and the constituted armed forces of the United States. Such a connection could jeopardize the possibility of further covert operations, not to mention our own political careers. If Barrabas has somehow put you up to making this request on his behalf, I'm afraid you're going to have to tell him no. He's on his own."

"Barrabas didn't put me up to anything," Jessup said. "I'm acting without his knowledge or consent."

"Then you should have known better."

There wasn't anything more to be said.

Jessup couldn't stand being in the same room with the senator any longer. The way the lawmaker was smiling made him want to break bones.

Slowly. Into very tiny pieces.

"Thanks for nothing," Jessup said, storming out the door.

It had been a long shot, all right. He'd known that going in. But if he could have gotten the senator's okay, he might have actually talked Barrabas into it. Now there was nothing to be done. It was all up to fate.

He lumbered past the secretary. She was back at the video game, hard at work trying to top her personal best score of four out of a possible 500,000. Once again she pretended that he did not exist.

It was one of the two things she was good at.

7

Barrabas raised the phone to his ear like a loaded gun, gingerly and with profound respect. "Who the hell is this?" he snarled.

From the earpiece came the hiss and crackle of an international connection. Then a voice that spoke as if it was submerged. Not in water but something much deeper.

Corn syrup.

Motor oil.

"Colonel, it's Billy."

The words came out torturously slow, as if the stringing of them together was a task of supreme effort. Barrabas did not recognize the voice.

"Bullshit!" he shouted into the phone. "Billy's dead. Who is this?"

"I'm not dead. Yet."

"Prove it."

There was a long silence at the other end of the line. For a moment Barrabas thought the sick practical joker had gotten tired of the game and hung up. Then the voice spoke again.

"Vince Biondi drove the truck."

"So?"

"He drove it one-way."

The white-haired man grimaced as if struck in the gut. The reference was to the Iran mission. Nobody but the SOBs knew Vince Biondi's last crazy selfless act on earth. It was their secret and theirs alone. It was Billy Two, all right. He was alive and a captive. His captors were undoubtedly listening in on the conversation.

"Are you okay?" Barrabas asked him. "You don't sound good."

"I'm okay. They want something."

Barrabas figured as much. "What is it?"

"They want to meet on Majorca. At Dr. Lee's place. They say they'll give me back in exchange for a talk."

"That's real sportsmanlike of them, but we don't have anything to talk about."

"They say they do."

"A meet with me, alone?"

There was a pause.

"With everybody."

"How soon?"

"Two days. Three days."

"I'll see what I can do."

"Thanks, Colonel."

"Hang in, Billy."

The line went dead.

Barrabas stared at the purring receiver in his hand.

"Well?" Gunther said. "Was it really him? Is he really alive?"

"Yeah, he's alive. Drugged to the gills. But alive."

"That's great news!"

Barrabas knew different. "Spetsnaz is using him as bait. They want all the SOBs on Majorca for a 'talk.' If we go willingly into the trap they say they'll let Billy go."

"What are we going to do?"

The white-haired man smiled. "Majorca's as good a place as any to die."

8

Dr. Leona Hatton put down her copy of the *International Herald-Tribune*. She set it beside her untouched cup of coffee. Coffee gone cold. For the second time in less than a week there was a coded personal ad in the classified section directed at her and the other SOBs.

The first ad had said: "Uncle Gridley plans a visit soon." It was the agreed-upon warning that GRU was making its move on them. The second ad that had appeared in that morning's paper was Barrabas's standard summons for the all of the SOBs to rendezvous ASAP at their training base, the doctor's rural Balearic island retreat, Ca'n Hatton, *Ca'n* being a Majorcan contraction of the Spanish *Casa d'En*.

It was not the contents of the ads that bothered Dr. Lee; it was their sequence. It told her that Barrabas had decided to make a stand, knowing full well what the outcome would be. It was the same decision she would have made. To go down swinging. She was glad she hadn't taken the mercenary leader's advice and left the ramshackle sixteenth-century Majorcan farmhouse she had inherited from her father, the general. If she had gone, she would've missed the almond blossoms.

The pretty, black-haired lady rose from her seat at the scarred, rough-hewn oak table. She shivered. It was cold and damp in the big empty house, a result of a popular Majorcan folk myth subscribed to by generations of island architects and builders. According to the myth, winter on Majorca simply didn't exist. All the old stone houses were built with that idea in mind. Central heating was unheard of. The doors and windows fit so badly they let drafts of frigid air sweep from one end of the house to the other.

Much of the time, it was warmer outside the casa than in.

She walked out onto the veranda under the latticework of an arbor that supported heavily branched but winter-dormant vines. Below her, carved out of the steep side of the mountain, were the grounds of her late father's estate. The rows of terraces stair-stepping down the slope were supported by natural-stone retaining walls that cut irregular but pleasing lines across the hill face. The road leading up to the main house zigged and zagged through six needle-sharp hairpins, through the groves of blooming almond trees. A sea of delicate white and pink blossoms. White for bitter fruit, pink for sweet. A sight that leaped out and caressed the eye, the heart.

General Hatton hadn't done any of the elaborate terrace landscaping; that, like the main house, was centuries old. Lee's father had bought the *estancia* as a retirement home but had died before he ever moved in.

Somehow that didn't matter to her. She had always felt his presence in this place, with its sweeping view of the narrow, partially cultivated valley; the jagged, towering backdrop of La Serra, a mountain ridge that jutted up directly behind the main house.

Dr. Lee took in the blaze of color, and a lump rose in her throat. She was not thinking about the likelihood of her own death; she was thinking about the death of her father's dream. With an effort she shook off the smothering feeling of sadness, the sense of personal failure. The estate had stood through four hundred years of intermittent conflict. It was part of the mountain, timeless, immutable. It had been the inspiration for the dreams of countless men. And would inspire countless more.

She turned back to the house. There was much to do before the others arrived.

CLAUDE HAYES JOGGED up the narrow crushed-cinder road. The valley's long, gradual grade was deceptive. So easy on the way down, so hard on the way back. Even though he ran the Majorcan road five days a week, he got the pain in his calves and thighs at exactly the same spot every time. He called it the hurting tree. A gnarled and ancient olive two-thirds of the way back to Ca'n Hatton.

This morning a tiny lady dressed all in black sat perched on the stone wall beneath the hurting tree. Her face bore the wrinkles of more than eighty years of life; she was toothless, but the infirmities of age had not dimmed her mind. She waved at the tall, muscular black man and smiled.

Hayes stopped running, even though he hadn't finished his workout. He leaned against the wall and caught his breath. The people of the valley thought he was crazy for busting his butt, rain or shine on the stretch of rough road, and they told him so at every possible opportunity. He had taken an instant liking to both the island and its people, or at least to most of them. They were farmers, simple, dignified, generous to a fault. They believed in the therapeutic value of hard physical work. When they caught him running for fun, they invariably offered to let him enjoy himself repairing their stone terraces, pruning their fruit trees. Sometimes he took them up on it, when he knew they really needed the help to get by. Not that there wasn't plenty of back-breaking labor to be had at Ca'n Hatton. Half-assed repairs made by people who knew nothing about construction or plumbing created some truly spectacular problems four centuries later.

"How are you, today, Mrs. Llonga?" he said, speaking in the island's dialect, lisping Castilian

Spanish with a smattering of Arabic words thrown in.

"No worse, thank you, Mr. Hayes," she said. "I see you are perspiring heavily. You must be having especially good fun today."

"You're right."

"Did you solve the problem with your water system?"

Claude shook his head. Drops of sweat fell from his face to the dusty road. "I'll sort it all out by this evening, though, I am sure."

"Confidence is a wonderful thing," she said. "Especially in the face of history's lessons."

"I don't understand."

"That reservoir hasn't worked properly for 250 years, since the day it was installed. They say the architect was not of the island."

"That would explain it, then," Hayes said with a straight face. He looked over the little woman's shawl-wrapped head, up the valley to the pink-and-white slopes. Everything was so peaceful all the time here. There was a comforting regularity, a flow to the labor, to the passing of the seasons. It was such a real place and yet so unreal to a man like Hayes, a professional soldier bloodied in the wars of Southeast Asia, and later, Africa. It was the kind of place he longed in his soul to be part of, a place where death rarely came to the young and where, to the old, it was a comfort, not a terror.

It was the past.

"You seem troubled, Mr. Hayes," Mrs. Llonga said.

"No, ma'am," he lied. "But I do think I'd better get back to the well before the day slips away. It might take another 250 years to fix it."

"A nice, steady job for generations of the family Hayes."

"I'm a better plumber than that, I hope."

"Nothing stays fixed forever. Or broken, either."

Claude said goodbye and pushed away from the wall, resuming his jog uphill. He paid for the short rest stop. His legs had tightened up. They did not want to run anymore. What they wanted wasn't important to him. He drove himself past the pain and into the steady groove of effort, breathing, peace.

The news about Spetsnaz closing in hadn't surprised him. He had known all along that his stay in the idyllic Majorcan valley wouldn't last. He had known he wasn't going to be able to grow old here, old and gnarled like the hurting tree, wrinkled and wise like Grandmother Llonga. That made every minute, every breath he took, more precious.

He drew the fragrance of almond blossom deep into his lungs and kicked for home.

9

The dining hall of Ca'n Hatton with its massive open-beam ceiling, its water-damaged, warped but still beautiful inlaid parquet floor, its huge, beehive-shape fireplace, had on the eves of other hazardous, virtually suicidal missions been a place of laughter, jokes à la Grand Guignol, true camaraderie. On this eve of battle, however, the faces of the assembled Soldiers of Barrabas were uniformly grim. No one spoke. They hardly looked at one another. All were waiting for their leader to break the oppressive silence.

The white-haired man stood mute at the head of the long, ancient oak table. He wasn't waiting for the right moment to begin. He was searching for the right words.

"We all knew it would come to this," he told them, looking from face to face. "When we met in this room two months ago, before the gulag mission, I explained the probable unpleasant consequences to you. And I gave you each the chance to back out of the job with no shame attached. None of you got up and left. Maybe I'm reading you guys wrong, reading my own feelings into yours, but I think, deep down, we all wanted things to turn out exactly as they have. I know I wanted to go up against Spetsnaz. To go head to head—to the finish. To see just how good they really are.''

"To show them just how fucking good *we* are," O'Toole said.

"It's the death wish, pure and simple," Nate Beck added matter-of-factly. The undersize, underweight electronics and computer genius knew what he was talking about. He was the SOB with the least firefight experience, the weakest combat skills, without a doubt the most vulnerable of any of them, but when it came to hard-charging into the teeth of battle he took a back seat to no one. Of the eight SOBs in the room, his death wish was by far the best developed.

"I don't think you have to worry about reading us wrong, Colonel," Nanos said, turning to address the others. "Am I right?"

Heads nodded all around.

A wide grin split the swarthy pie-face of Chank Dayo, the Inuit bush pilot and war buddy of Billy Two who had flown them out of Siberia. "If we were interested in short odds," he said, "we'd all still be in the service, Colonel."

"Or working for the post office," Hayes suggested.

"Same thing," O'Toole said.

Barrabas smiled. Not a crybaby in the lot.

"Shouldn't you tell them the news before we elect a yell king?" Dr. Lee asked him.

Her sarcasm wrung a chorus of groans from the others. Things were back to normal in the SOBs' briefing room.

"Billy Two is alive," he said.

The announcement caught the SOBs flat-footed. They all shut up and stared in shock at Barrabas.

"Not funny," Nanos said angrily, pushing up from his chair. "Not funny at all."

O'Toole clapped a hand on the Greek's rock-hard shoulder, stepping between him and the colonel. "Easy, now," he said. "Let's allow the man to finish what he has to say."

"Go ahead," Nanos said. "Finish it."

"I'm sorry, Alex. I know losing Billy hit you the hardest. What I've got to say isn't going to make you feel any better. I know it sure as hell made me feel worse. Billy is alive. I talked to him on the phone the day before yesterday."

"That's fucking impossible!" Beck exclaimed.

"Colonel," Chank said, "all of us on that gulag runway saw him get hit."

"It doesn't matter what you saw or I saw or what we thought we saw," Barrabas said. "I talked to Billy. It was him, there was no doubt of it. Spetsnaz has him. They're holding him prisoner."

Nanos dropped back into his chair. "Holy shit," he muttered, shaking his head.

"I told you the news wouldn't make things easier. The chances of our freeing Starfoot or ever setting eyes on him again are slim and none. He told me Spetsnaz wanted to talk with us here at Dr. Lee's place. He said they would let him go if we agreed to parley."

"What a load of Commie horseshit," O'Toole growled. "How dumb do they think we are?"

"Did Billy sound all right?" Nanos asked.

"Drugged. Other than that I couldn't tell."

"No way we can locate him?"

Barrabas shook his head. "We've got no intel on anything Spetsnaz is doing or about to do. We can only deduce and take our best shot."

"A hard, fast strike, that's what they'll shoot for," O'Toole said with conviction. "In and out before the *guardia civile* know what hit them."

"Hit us," Hayes corrected.

"Yeah. Us."

"Liam's right," Gunther interjected. "Even on Majorca, where there's no threat of a heavy-duty police response, Spetsnaz is going to want to get everything over quick, with minimum fuss—if for no other reason than to make it easier for them all to get off the island."

"So, you're saying all we have to do is turn back their first all-out blitz and they'll roll over?" Dayo asked.

"No," Barrabas answered. "These guys will keep at it as long as it takes, even if they have to battle government troops from the Spanish mainland. They want us that badly. No matter what, we should be able to hold our own against them for at least the first few hours. Thanks to Walter Jessup and his connections, we have been suitably armed."

"The fat man sends his regrets," O'Toole informed them.

"Also a dozen Armalites," Gunther said. "Ammo, frag grenades, side arms and enough C-4 to bring down half the mountain."

"Gee, I wonder why he couldn't make this one?" Nanos asked sourly.

"Our defense of Dr. Lee's estate is not going to be complicated," Barrabas said, unfolding a large-scale map he had sketched earlier in the day. He tacked the map to the wall, then started pointing out features of interest. "Problem areas we should all be aware of," he said, "are the ridge spires of La Serra rising directly behind and three hundred feet above the main house. If we lose control of the high ground, the strongest point of our defense, I guarantee you it's going to be a very short, very dull campaign for Spetsnaz. The narrow terraces leading downslope are natural barriers to penetration, but they would work more in our favor if it wasn't almond blossom time. There's too damn much cover for Spetsnaz to slip through. We can defend the terrace walls but we aren't going to be able to see the opposition coming until they're looking right up our noses.''

"What about the road, Colonel?" Dr. Lee said.

He told her what she already knew. "We don't have enough manpower to guard every hairpin.''

"That means mining it with C-4," she said evenly.

Barrabas shook his head. "I'm keeping all the plastic explosive up here." He addressed the entire group. "I've never bullshitted any of you and I'm sure as hell not going to start now. We've got the chance to acquit ourselves honorably, to make Spetsnaz pay for the privilege of dancing with us. That's all.''

Silence once again fell over the group. The gut feelings of each had been confirmed: winning was a long shot not even worth mentioning.

"They've conceded choice of turf for the contest," Barrabas said. "Obviously, they don't think it will make any difference in the outcome. In my opinion, that was mistake number one. We've trained here for a half-dozen missions over the past year. We know this ground, inch by inch. And that's just how we're going to give it up.''

"And you guys thought I was kicking your butts over it just for fun," O'Toole said, grinning.

"Yeah, we really misjudged you," Beck said without force.

"Will you ever forgive us?" Nanos asked.

O'Toole gave them a one-finger salute.

"The idea," Barrabas told them, "is to hold position as long as possible, then fight in retreat to the casa."

"And the C-4," Dr. Lee said.

Nanos nudged O'Toole. "I've always wanted to go out with a bang," he confided.

"It's not that kind of bang, you asshole."

"We go on round-the-clock alert from now on," Barrabas told them. "You all know what that means with an eight-member team."

"Nobody sleeps," Hayes said.

Barrabas went on. "Liam and I have already worked out the duty assignments and rotation. You'll pick up your assignment with your weapons. O'Toole?"

The red-haired man nodded. "All right, folks, let's retire to the front foyer and crack some crates."

IN THE FEEBLE HALF-LIGHT of a waning moon, Leona Hatton and Alex Nanos scaled the crumbling limestone ridge. So sheer was the face of the mountain that the climb was almost vertical, a ladder ascent. They moved quickly, but not recklessly, burdened by Colt-made assault rifles slung by web straps over their backs, by clusters of hand grenades, by day packs crammed with loaded 40-round magazines. Neither of them looked down.

"If it's any consolation," Dr. Lee said softly as she reached overhead, stretching on tiptoe, feeling out a handhold with her fingertips, "this is the easy way up. If Spetsnaz wants to take the ridge line of La Serra, they're going to have to come from the north, the side facing the sea. The north side is a real bitch."

"Yeah, thanks, Doc, that makes my knees feel a whole lot better," Nanos said to the backs of her heels.

"Don't give me that bull," Lee told him. "You're not even breathing hard. You're in shape, for a change. What happened, did it finally fall off in your hand?"

"No, Doc, it was my hand that fell off."

"That must've been a relief to all the bimbos in Teaneck."

"Yeah, but it sure shot the shit out of the plans to raise a memorial statue on the Turnpike."

"Would have been a nice gesture."

"Hey, we're talking class act! A thirty-foot-high, concrete-and-steel, nude rendering of Nanos the Greek, from midthigh to navel, buns to Baltimore, balls to Brooklyn."

"A mecca for the cocktail waitresses of the world," Lee said, then she abruptly changed the subject. "Alex, we've got some tricky parts ahead here. These ledges are all half-rotten rock. Watch it."

"Right."

Free climbing wasn't the Greek's idea of a good time, but the tricky parts certainly occupied every ounce of his concentration and kept his mind off the resurrection of William Starfoot II. When they reached the 2000-foot summit of La Serra's highest point, his mind fell back into the shallow groove it had worn for itself. He stood on edge of the windswept, lightning-blasted peak, staring down at the dark and narrow valley below. Staring without seeing.

Dr. Lee sensed his discomfort. She knew the cause.

"You never know what's going to happen, Alex," she told him, putting her hand on his shoulder. "Billy just might beat them yet. At least he's got a chance now. Before, when we all thought he'd bought the ranch at Tarkotovo, all the possibilities for him had run out."

Nanos looked her straight in the eye. "I know you're just trying to help and I hope you'll forgive me for saying it, Doc, but the bright side of Billy's situation purely sucks. There are worse things than being dead. And one of them is to be tortured by experts. Guys who know how to take somebody to the limit and hold them dangling there for days."

Dr. Lee was glad it was dark on the mountaintop so Nanos couldn't see the embarrassment burning in her cheeks. They were all backed up against the execution wall and there she was, playing Pollyanna.

She put her face into the cutting edge of the wind and thought about worse things than being dead.

10

Billy Two lay strapped on his back to yet another bed, this one much smaller and occupied by the previous tenants who refused to be evicted. He watched the shiny brown cockroach scamper up the wall beside his head. It was a big sucker, like a cigar butt with three-inch-long legs. It ran almost all the way up to the twelve-foot ceiling before launching itself in a graceful back flip. It landed on his forehead with a stinging smack and then ran down the bridge of his nose, across his cheek to nuzzle affectionately in the sweaty hollow of his neck.

Other specimens of brown vermin, smaller ones, were likewise literally climbing the walls to dive-bomb him.

It was the cockroach Olympics.

The room he was confined to was hardly bigger than the sheetless single-bed mattress he lay on. He looked up at the ceiling, crazed with thousands of cracks. Hundreds of thousands. It had been painted over so many times that if the layered paint fell, its weight alone would have been enough to crush him flat. There was an

open window just above his head. It looked out
onto the tiny, gritty inner courtyard of the Barcelona tenement. Smells from outside rushed over
him in an unbroken wave.

Garbage, yes.

Undisposed-of disposable diapers, yes.

But above all, home permanent.

It smelled as though the entire female popula-
tion of the slum building was in curlers, indulg-
ing in a veritable orgy of hair-styling.

Voices came from the other room. Male
voices. Billy didn't understand what they were
saying. His captors always talked in Russian
when there was no one else around. Billy Two
counted as no one in their book. He was a mind-
less slab of beef to be hauled around, strapped
down on the bed so he wouldn't fall out and hurt
himself. They fed and watered him, but grudg-
ingly and at infrequent intervals.

Things had improved for him since the move
from the Serbsky Institute. They had cut out the
sulfur-drug therapy altogether. It made him too
violent to control outside the hospital setting.
And they had also cut back the dosage on his
pink injections so he could almost walk without
help, so he could pass through customs check-
points without drawing undue attention to himself. He was actually much stronger than he let
on. Either his tolerance for the drugs was building or his resolve to fight their effects, at least in-
wardly, was working. Placid on the outside, a

six-foot-six mahogany-colored Kewpie doll, the Indian's mind seethed with near-constant rage.

The big roach tickled his earlobe with its forelegs, then climbed aboard and made itself at home, taking a seat, preening its long antennae.

Billy started to shake his head to try and dislodge the creature when it spoke to him. Not in words. In thoughts.

"Soon, Starfoot," the roach said.

He recognized the voice. "Hawk Spirit, is that you?"

"Yes."

Billy relaxed on the lumpy mattress. Hawk Spirit had come to him in many guises over the past few days. A fat concierge with nylons rolled down around her blotched and bloated ankles. A tiny gray-brown bird that sat on the sill above his head. Each time he had come and gone Billy had gotten stronger. The spirit of the Osage did nothing tangible to him or for him; there were no lessons in the usual sense. They just talked and afterward he could never remember what had been said, only that it made him feel much better. And that afterward, when he focused his fury on his enemies, he felt better still.

"Soon, Starfoot," Hawk Spirit told him, "your opportunity will come. You must seize it without hesitation. It will not come again."

"How will I know it?"

"How do you know your own hand?"

"By its shape. Because it is connected to me."

"This opportunity is like a part of you that has been severed and taken away. When you and it are reunited you will recognize each other."

"You have led me through the fire under the skin. Past the place where air is thick like syrup. Will you guide me farther? To the end?"

"I have come as far as I can. You must do the fighting. I am smoke."

"Will there be much blood?"

"Much blood."

Billy lay on his back on the crawling bed, his eyes unblinking, staring unfocused at the ceiling, the muscles of his face slack like dead meat. Except for the corners of his mouth. Under the white crust of dried spittle, a tiny smile flickered.

11

Balandin sat stiffly upright in an armchair, his shoulders wrapped with a light blanket, watching day break over the Bay of Palma. On the other side of the floor-to-ceiling windows of the eighth-story Paseo Sagrera flat, gray clouds drifted above a mercury-colored sea; white yachts bobbed, white gulls wheeled before his burning eyes. Around his bare feet, scattered across the shag carpet, were plastic-wrapped, heavily-greased AK-74s, heaps of extra loaded 30-round box magazines, stilettos, RDG-5 anti-personnel grenades, RPG-7s, webbed battle harnesses. He had sat there the whole night, amid the instruments of his profession, unable to sleep. Since his accident he had slept very little. He did not like his dreams. They not only replayed in clinical detail the moment of his castration but turned its aftermath like some vast multifaceted stone to display unforeseen, unimagined consequences. Some were in the nature of animated public-toilet graffiti, crude Freudian cartoons. Others were more subtle, involving his forgetting his infirmity, making a sexual liaison with a woman, only to rediscover his loss at the crucial moment and before a highly amused audience.

He saw no irony in the manner of his unmanning, that a woman had robbed him, the rapist, the batterer, of the use of his most prized weapon. In his castration he saw only the grossest, the ultimate of injustices. There was no righting such a wrong, such a lightly, off-handedly performed wrong; no comparable injury he could inflict on the black-haired bitch. All he could do was kill her. Kill her as slowly as possible. With the maximum amount of pain. He had toyed with many fantasies of vengeance. His current favorite had a local flavor. There was a town on Majorca called San Telmo, after Saint Elmo, who achieved martyrdom after his stomach had been slashed open and his bowels tied to, then cranked out and around a windlass. A windlass, of course, would be hard to find at a target like Ca'n Hatton, so many miles away from the ships and the harbor, but that wasn't important anyway. It was the operating principle that interested Balandin, not the precise duplication of the machinery employed on the ancient Christian. There were always mechanical substitutes available. If not an electric-powered winch, then one of the drive wheels of a jacked-up car. Or even a bicycle.

A soft noise from behind, the sound of a cautious footstep muffled by the deep-pile carpet made Balandin jerk to attention in his chair.

"Sorry to have disturbed you, Captain," said the small, frail man in the flannel pajamas and light-blue terry-cloth bathrobe.

Balandin scowled at Vladimir Tkach and said nothing. Tkach was the civilian GRU agent-in-place on Majorca. Up until four days previously, he had received a sizable salary for doing next to nothing. When pressed by distant superiors he had occasionally provided a little photographic surveillance on the U.S. radar station on Majorca. He had also made feeble attempts to spy on vacationing foreign and armed service personnel, noting potential targets and avenues for blackmail. Nothing that could have been considered the least bit hazardous to his health. Until now.

Vladimir Tkach had done the job asked of him, all right, despite the danger. He had provided all fifty-eight of the Spetsnaz attack force with safe houses, maps, transport on and escape routes from the island. He had done it because he was afraid not to.

That didn't mean he liked the idea.

"Captain, why is it necessary for there to be two diversions here in Palma prior to the main assault inland?" the small man whined. "Surely one would succeed in drawing the attention of the island police."

Balandin turned away from the man without

bothering to answer, folding his arms across his chest, staring pointedly out the windows.

"Two attacks make no sense to me," the agent-in-place protested.

The captain turned back slowly, glaring. Clearly he was not going to be left alone. "Chaos, you stupid bastard," he said in a voice chillingly devoid of emotion. "Palma will be ripped end to end. The streets will run with blood. One catastrophe the *guardia* might be able to handle, to contain, but never two. Never two so widely separated."

Tkach grimaced and swallowed hard.

Balandin could see how the soft and easy life on the Balearic island had thoroughly corrupted the already weak Tkach. The agent-in-place purely hated to see his little paradise disrupted, his cozy Mediterranean nest shaken. The captain made a mental note to pull strings when he returned to Moscow, to get the man transferred to a different duty station in a less desirable locale. Greenland, perhaps, or even Canada.

Tkach continued to stand there, shifting his weight from one slippered foot to the other, wringing his soft, pale hands, looking both helpless and pathetic. The sight of him was more than Balandin could take.

"Go wet your bed," the captain said.

The agent-in-place stiffened. "What?" he asked.

"That's an order," Balandin barked.

Only after the man scurried out of the room did the captain crack a smile. He wondered if the worm Tkach would bother to take off his pajamas before he did his duty to the motherland.

Balandin checked his wristwatch. It was almost half past six. He knew by this time the anvil group, Sergeant Ilin and her eleven men, should have already landed at the beach on the north side of the island. By now Ilin would be staring up at the sheer limestone cliffs, cursing him. Again, the captain found reason to smile. He had given the female GRU squad leader the hardest of all the jobs related to the mission. She had to take her equipment-laden team almost straight up, then up and down, over the bleached, craggy peaks until they reached the high ground directly behind Ca'n Hatton. It was the hardest job, but Sergeant Ilin would do it perfectly, as much to spite him as to avenge her service's honor.

The other components of Balandin's attack plan for the SOB stronghold were already assembled and poised to begin the assault at his command. The diversionary unit, led by Sergeant Munshin, was billeted a scant quarter-mile from its twin targets. While Ilin and the anvil group laboriously worked their way into position there was nothing for the rest of the Spetsnaz force to do but wait. For their leader, there was one simple task left to perform.

Balandin rose from the armchair, letting the blanket slip from his shoulders and fall to the rug. He walked over to the apartment's telephone, picked up the handset and dialed a Barcelona number. It was time for the Amerind SOB to join his doomed comrades in spirit. And in parts.

12

The pair of Spetsnaz soldiers pulled Billy Two from the tiny bed, hauling him to his feet. The brown man did not resist them. He appeared to be without motive power of his own, a thing made of wax. Once bent into a position, he remained that way until twisted in some other direction.

The catatonic appearance was an act. Behind the dull eyes, Billy Two's mind was running at redline, operating with a clarity, an intensity it had never known before, not only supercharged, but supersensitized. With it, he could *feel* the depth and breadth of every crack in the wall opposite; with it, he could *feel* every single layer of peeling paint on the wooden door.

His captors gathered up his clothes. The trooper with the half-smoked cigarette dangling from his lips dragged a T-shirt down over Billy's head while the other man wrestled with his trousers, the right leg of which had been slashed from ankle to hip to accommodate the heavy plaster cast. They were so confident of their ability to control him that they treated him almost casually—a pair of butch window dressers mauling a department-store dummy.

As the smoker drew back, a slender finger of gray ash dropped from his cigarette onto Billy's bare forearm. A week before he had been so tranquilized he would not have even felt the heat. Today he felt both heat and impact.

They did not bother to tie his hands or further hobble his feet. There was no reason to. In the cast, Billy Two could barely walk without their support. The Spetsnaz soldiers exited the grim two-room flat holding the crippled brown man propped between them.

The corridor outside was deserted. As they dragged him along, Billy Two's feet made a scraping sound on the mosaic-tile floor, the design of which was obscured by decades of undisturbed grime. He gave them no help whatsoever, forcing them to bear his entire weight. The troopers staggered with their burden down the broad stairs. By the time they reached the courtyard and its open-air parking area they were sweating profusely.

They shoved Billy Two against the hood of a dark-blue Ford Escort four-door. The smoker unlocked one of the rear doors and then he and his comrade crammed the Indian into the back seat. Because of the cast and his necessarily outstretched right leg it was impossible for one of the Spetsnaz soldiers to join him in the back seat; he took up all the room there was. They locked him in, then climbed into the front of the car.

As the man driving started up the Escort, his heavily nicotine-addicted partner lit up another cigarette, using a disposable butane lighter. The trooper had the lighter's flame set way too high. A three-inch dagger of blue leaped up to kindle the business end of the unfiltered Benson & Hedges. With a squirm of his lips, the smoker rolled the ignited cigarette into its rightful place in the corner of his mouth. He dragged deep on it, his cheeks hollowing. When he exhaled, he did so over the back of his seat, right into Billy Two's face.

The Indian coughed and turned his head. There was no getting away from the stink, though. All the windows were tightly rolled up. In a matter of seconds it was like a cesspit in the back of the car.

The Escort eased forward, under the overhang of the entry arch. The driver stopped the car short of the tall, double wooden doors barring the exit to the street. He honked his horn until the concierge waddled out and opened them.

Outside, the streets of Barcelona were already clogged with morning traffic. The driver used the compact Ford like a weapon, levering his way into the flow of cars and trucks. In the shallow canyon of ancient stone-faced buildings the air was choked with swirling particles, a by-product of diesel exhausts. The building fronts were all a uniform, dull black, coated with auto soot and oil. The streets were likewise black—not dull, but shiny. This wasn't because of diesel dirt; they were paved with rough-hewn slabs of black rock.

The Ford crept along for a few blocks, then turned onto a side street and again onto another main avenue, just as congested but much classier. Well-to-do Spaniards strolled the sidewalk not three feet from where Billy Two sat. The potbellied men in barber-style shirt jackets, the women in gaudy, slut-chic makeup and Italian fashions, paid no attention to him. A cry for help would have turned their heads, but only long enough to measure the source and reject it. The man in the back seat of the Escort was definitely not Spanish, and more to the point, not in style.

As the traffic inched ahead, the Spetsnaz troopers joked back and forth in the front seat, certain that their captive could not understand their words. It was a correct assumption. What little Russian Billy Two had managed to pick up over the past weeks was of no use to him. They were speaking so quickly he couldn't tell where one word ended and the next began. That did not keep him from clearly reading their intent.

This was to be his last ride.

On the floor of the car next to his right foot, partially shoved under the driver's seat, was a cloth bag with a drawstring. Its contents protruded slightly from the slack opening. A handle. A polished walnut handle with a brass-lined hole and a short, leather wrist thong. Billy could see the shape of the thing beneath the cloth. It was not just a knife, it was a cleaver. A heavy cleaver. He recognized its type. The razor-honed blade would be wedge-shaped, instead of hollow ground. The kind of instrument meat cutters use to disjoint the carcasses of large animals. A spine-splitter. A pelvis-cracker.

His usefulness to them at an end, Spetsnaz was hauling him off to slaughter. And they were going to dismember him. The only question was: would they kill him first?

Billy Two's knuckles turned white as he gripped the edge of the bench seat. The urge to do mayhem was almost more than he could control. The handle of the cleaver was easily within his reach. He knew he could deliver a killing blow to either the driver or the smoker. He also knew that the man he chose to ignore would shoot him dead where he sat. The urge was there, but the opportunity was not right. He shook off the crimson haze of rage, content to wait for the moment Hawk Spirit had promised him. The moment he would recognize.

He turned his mind to other things—things he had not been able to think about in his drug stupor. He wondered if by now GRU had already taken its revenge on the Soldiers of Barrabas? Had all his friends been destroyed? Was he an afterthought, the last bit of bothersome refuse to be flicked away? A small smile lit up his unshaved, unwashed brown face. Warriors like Nile Barrabas, Liam O'Toole and the others were not easy to kill. They died hard, died mean. Annihilating them, no matter what the odds, would be a tall order.

Tall and costly.

The Indian's smile broadened. And if there was a way for the SOBs to win, to survive, the colonel would find it. Billy Two considered his own survival, what he would do, where he would go if he managed to escape his executioners. It didn't require much thought. For him, there was only one choice. Majorca and Ca'n Hatton. To bury his comrades if necessary, to die fighting beside them if he could.

The driver of the Escort uttered a sigh of relief as he pointed out their destination to the smoker. Then he gunned the engine savagely and spun the wheel hard over, creating a space between two cars in the right lane where no space had been. Horns bleated, clenched fists appeared out of rolled-down windows. The Spetsnaz driver laughed and continued to the right, into a narrow drive very similar to the one they had just left. It was barely long enough for the car and it ended in a grimy, stone building front and archway. The entrance was blocked by double wooden doors.

The man behind the wheel got out and ran to the padlock and chain on the doors. He unlocked the chain and swung the doors inward, then returned to the car. As they started to roll forward into the dimness, he turned on the Escort's headlights.

There was a built-in workbench along the back wall. On it were scattered tin cans, empty bottles. Whatever the concrete-floored area had once been, it was abandoned now. There were two small windows set high in the left-hand wall, but they were so heavily caked with grime that they passed only a weak yellow light.

The driver stopped the car and got out again, running to close the double doors behind them. The smoker jumped out, too, and opened the passenger-side rear door. He raised the foot of the cast over the doorjamb, then gestured for Billy to scoot forward, toward him.

Billy blinked back, a dazed look on his face.

Muttering a curse, the smoker stormed around to the other side of the car, opened the other door, then leaned into the back seat. He grabbed hold of the back of the waistband of the Indian's trousers and pulled for all he was worth.

Starfoot permitted himself to be slid backward across the seat. When he was about to be dumped out on his butt, he reached up and grabbed the gutter of the car roof.

"Let go!" the smoker snarled.

Billy Two refused.

The Spetsnaz trooper did not ask twice. He hit Billy's knuckles with the edge of his hand, smashing them against the car roof and the upraised gutter.

Starfoot let go.

And toppled out onto cement on his backside, his cast catching in under the passenger seat, leaving him helpless on the ground. With more and louder curses, the smoker bent down to free him. Then the driver joined him and both of them raised the Indian to his feet. They pushed him up against the rear fender and left him leaning over the trunk lid while they took a quick meeting at the other end of the car.

His captors out of the way, Billy carefully surveyed the intended place of his execution. The movable furnishings were concentrated against the wall directly behind him. They consisted of a few wooden crates and a litter of paper, empty tins and larger metal containers, paint buckets, gallon cans. Next to these there was a washstand. The frame of the mirror above it was empty of glass, the sink stained with streaks the color of motor oil. On the edge of the sink was a roll of toilet paper. A very old roll. Because of the damp it had swollen up to twice normal size. The most important fixture in the room was on the floor—a six-inch drain set in the concrete.

Starfoot straightened up and began to move.

Carefully pivoting on his stiff leg, he shuffled through the debris, his arms outstretched to keep his balance.

The Spetsnaz troopers regarded him with amused curiosity, but made no move to stop him. Even if he could have run, with the doors locked there was no place for him to go. The smoker took a long last drag on his cigarette, then ground it out under his heel.

Billy Two struggled to the filthy sink. Exactly as Hawk Spirit had predicted, he recognized the place, the objects. And not only that, he had an unshakable feeling he was about to do something he had already done once before. He cranked both of the water taps open, though he knew no water was going to come out. Behind him the troopers laughed at what they thought was his disappointment.

As he half turned to look at them over his shoulder, he pushed the roll of toilet paper into the sink. The driver stepped away from his comrade, heading for the stack of crates along the wall. One of them would serve as a chopping block. They would place it next to the drain, then haul their unprotesting victim over its edge, one of them holding him by the hair, stretching his neck taut while the other hacked and hacked until the head dropped free. The smoker returned to the back seat of the Escort, leaning in and coming out with the cloth bag and the cleaver.

With difficulty Billy Two bent over and reached for the gallon-size red can with the handle on top. It was beside the washstand's pedestal. As he raised the container, its contents sloshed reassuringly. Putting his back to the troopers, he concealed what he was doing in the sink. As he twisted the metal lid open there was a whoosh of air, then the unmistakable odor of gasoline. It was the right can. He dumped the high-octane fuel into the sink, saturating the toilet-paper roll.

"What do you have there?" the driver demanded as he put a foot up on the crate he had just set in place.

"He's just playing a game," the smoker said, pulling the cleaver out of the cloth bag, testing its edge carefully with the ball of his thumb. "He's pretending to wash his hands." The smoker put the cleaver blade between his arm and side, trapping it there with his elbow. He stuck his fingers into his breast pocket and pulled out an opened packet of Benson & Hedges. "We have another game for you to play," he told Billy, shaking out a smoke, gripping it between his front teeth. "It's much more fun than washing your hands. Come over here and we'll show you."

Billy half turned again, his hand in the sink, his fist wrapped around the big, mushy wad of paper. He gave them his patented blank look.

The smoker pulled the lighter from his pocket

and held it beneath his chin. "Go and get him," he told the driver as he flicked the ignition wheel.

The three inches of blue flame licked up.

Before the driver could take a step, Billy Two swung his hand from the sink. Sidearm. The roll of toilet paper disintegrated as it flew, splattering over the smoker's face from forehead to throat.

The gas vapor ignited with a sucking rush.

The trooper's entire head was instantly a ball of fire. Arms flailing, he jumped back a full yard, as if to pull away from the flame.

He was the flame.

He beat his face with his open hands, his legs pistoning, his feet dancing a mad tattoo. The cleaver clattered to the concrete. The fire would not go out, no matter how he twisted or turned. The smoker's mouth gaped, a black hole as he prepared to scream. When he drew breath, he also drew burning gasoline deep into his lungs.

There was no scream.

Muscle, cartilage, mucous membrane, melding, flowing, useless, he had nothing left to scream with. His head a smoldering wreck, he fell back against the side of the car, then slumped to the floor.

The driver was so stunned, so shaken, he stood riveted in place.

Not so Billy Two. At the instant he released the gasoline spitball, the huge Indian hurled himself after it, away from the sink, toward the burning man. He hopped three giant steps before diving headfirst for the cleaver. Despite the jarring impact he got his fist around the handle. While the smoker burned, Billy Two rolled to his side and turned the heavy blade on himself, chopping insanely at his own right leg.

Which only increased the driver's confusion.

Starfoot wasn't trying to perform a self-amputation; he was trying to free himself from the cast. With a flurry of savage blows, he split the plaster shell like a crab claw, then ripped it apart with his hands. Before the driver could recover and draw his pistol, Billy Two had crawled out of sight, around the rear of the Escort.

The Indian knew as soon as he started to move that his leg hadn't been broken by the machine-gun slug in Siberia. The wound was clean, through and through the meat of his quad, and it had already healed perfectly. They had put him in the cast to hobble him, to make him easier to control.

There was no controlling him, now.

He heard the driver rounding the passenger side and scrambled the other way, past the left rear wheel, slithering under the car with his arms outstretched.

The driver quickly approached the Escort and his charred partner, his Makarov well out in front of him. He thought he was in good shape, ready for anything, but he wasn't ready for the two thick arms snaking suddenly out from under the car.

Billy Two seized him around the heels and jerked.

The driver let out a howl of surprise and pain as his shins impacted with the Escort's rocker panel, as he slammed to the concrete on his butt. The Makarov skipped away, out of reach. He howled even louder as those powerful hands started to pull, to keelhaul him under the car.

The Indian would not be denied. He dragged the screaming, thrashing trooper out feetfirst, grabbing handfuls of whatever to draw the man's head from under the rocker panel. Once he was clear, Billy Two kneeled on his chest, digging the fingers of his left hand deep into the man's throat. In his upraised right hand was the gleaming cleaver.

For a terrible moment their eyes locked, the panic-stricken member of Russia's finest and the wild-eyed mercenary. With a savage grunt, Billy Two swung the cleaver down. He swung hard—a killing blow—but death was not his only motive. His frenzy was such that it took a dozen similar licks to satisfy him. A dozen left the trooper's skull a caved-in shell and around it, on the concrete, a five-foot-wide halo of gore and bone chips.

Billy Two threw the cleaver aside. He fumbled in the dead man's jacket until he found the key to the doors, then he straightened up. He sniffed at the air and made a face. It smelled like a cross between a Texas pig roast and a fire in a felt factory.

Nothing to linger over.

He scooped up the pair of dropped Makarovs, unlocked and opened the doors, then ran back to the Escort. He started it up, turned it around with a squeal of tires, heading back out the drive and into traffic. For better or worse, Ca'n Hatton was only a ferryboat ride away.

13

Sergeant Munshin slid the stiletto's double-edged blade down the sharpening steel, first one side, then the other. He worked quickly, making the metal on metal sing. Every few seconds he paused to examine the full length of the blade. He was particularly careful with the pointed tip, taking great pains to make sure it was like a razor on both edges. When he was satisfied, he stroked the flat of the tip with his thumb. The blade hummed like a spring. Perfectly balanced, it felt almost alive in his hand. Almost as if it could leap forward on its own and skewer something. Something living. He slipped the stiletto back into its slim ankle sheath.

Munshin regarded the glow of the setting sun through the high window of his Terreno District hideaway with a scowl. The truth be known, the barrel-chested noncom did not much like his assignment for the evening. On a mission with so much potential for personal glory he had most certainly drawn the booby prize. While the other squad leaders were assaulting the American hooligans in their mountain stronghold, avenging the dishonor the SOBs had brought upon the leaders, upon the uniform of Spetsnaz, he and his ten-man team were stuck with the tedious chore of diverting the attention of the local police. For the Spetsnaz troopers, experts in urban terrorism, it was nothing more than a routine training exercise.

He rose from the edge of the bed and crossed the narrow room. Under the threadbare rug, the floor creaked mightily. It felt as if the boards were loose, not nailed down at all, just laid over the joists. Typical Spanish construction, he thought as he picked up the cake of camouflage makeup from the commode. Built of matchsticks by morons.

He applied the green grease in thin bands across his forehead and cheeks. Then he put a bold splotch on the point of his jutting chin. The camo was purely for shock effect. Theatrics. Divided in two assault teams, his men were going to attack a pair of public bars at opposite ends of the Plaza Gomila, the most concentrated tourist trap on the island. The only plant life they were going to be able to hide behind were the rubber trees in ceramic pots. The war paint made them *look* like terrorists, no-nonsense terrorists; it created the right impression, immediate respect and instantaneous fear.

Munshin checked his wristwatch. Still thirty minutes to go. Thirty minutes before he was to meet the truck out front. He returned to the rumpled bed, and for lack of anything better to do, began fieldstripping his AK-74.

He tried to rationalize the situation. Maybe it wasn't such a bad thing that he was taking a back seat on this job? Granted, he would miss the thrill of being there at the moment of the victory, but the others, the captain in particular, would know what he had sacrificed in order to ensure the success of the mission. A reputation as a team player was nothing to sneeze at. It could conceivably help him later on.

Munshin scowled again. He was feeding himself bullshit and he knew it. The system never claimed to be fair. Only the troopers with enemy blood on their boots would get the gravy and the limelight.

The sergeant's fingers flew, snapping the assault rifle back together in a series of crisp, precise operations. He cracked a loaded magazine into the weapon, then set it back on the foot of the bed.

As he leaned back against the bedstead, lacing his fingers behind his head, he knew there was only one real bright spot to the task at hand: he was going to get to kill some Brits.

14

Daylight was fading fast as Billy Two turned the commandeered Spetsnaz Ford down the winding, one-lane road from Valldemosa. Sunset's finale bathed the tops of the limestone peaks in red. The narrow valley ahead and below him was already steeped in deep shadow. He squirmed on the seat as he feathered the Escort's brakes, slowing for a hairpin right. Every inch of his skin prickled and itched maddeningly. Sweat trickled down the sides of his face. It wasn't a hot evening; the air was cool and getting cooler by the minute. Despite that, despite the fact that he had rolled the driver's window all the way down, the back of his shirt and the seat of his pants were both sticking to the car seat.

The heat came from within him; it was a fever of the mind. It came in waves. And when the waves peaked, his vision became distorted; the rocks and bushes at the sides of the road turned to a jittering sea of heads, some human, some animal, all with wildly staring eyes. The heat was such that he had an almost overpowering urge to tear all his clothes off, but he refused to give in to it. Instead he opened the air vent and angled the cool stream up at his face. It helped a little.

The road dropped quickly through a series of switchbacks. Because of the steep downgrade, he saw the flashing lights of the roadblock a full mile ahead. And seeing them, slammed on his brakes, growling a curse.

Was he already too late?

He pulled the car into a roadside *mirador* or viewing point, got out and stepped to the edge of the drop-off. Below him blue lights twirled on top of a white toy car. Billy Two glared at them for a full minute before the realization hit him.

Things were not as they seemed.

What did the roadblock mean? That the GRU hit had already gone down? He doubted it. Primarily because he knew how the *guardia civile* operated. They wouldn't shut down the road so far from the scene of the crime. If they were going to block anything, they would block the access drive to Ca'n Hatton. They were not much more than farm boys in uniform. They lacked the discipline and training to proceed in an orderly fashion after a traffic accident, never mind a multiple homicide. If there were *guardia* about, they would not be manning a roadblock; they would be up at the main house, playing Kojak, rolling over bodies, sniffing gun muzzles, destroying evidence.

If the roadblock wasn't official Majorcan,

then it was official GRU, sure as hell. And it meant that Spetsnaz hadn't struck, yet.

Billy Two jerked his gaze away from the spinning lights and shook his head to clear it. Before his eyes the blue flash-spot racing round and round the valley slopes had turned into an enormous snake, a snake chasing its own tail with dripping jaws agape. The heat billowed up inside him and suddenly he couldn't stand it any longer. As he rushed back to the Escort he ripped his shirtfront open, sending the buttons flying. He threw the shirt in the dirt, then leaned into the front of the car to gather his weapons. Sweat rolled down his chest, down the insides of his legs.

Going topless was not enough. Once he started, he could not stop himself. All the restraints had to go.

The pants came off, too.

And the jockey knits.

And the shoes and socks.

He left them all on the ground beside the car and, naked as the day he was born, set off down the road, a Makarov autopistol in either fist.

15

"Me, too," Nigel Dimmick said as the bartender drew a foamless pint of real ale for the fellow standing next to him at the bar. The Majorcan bartender smiled and nodded and pulled a second pint.

Nigel paid the tab, then swung the amber Theakston's to his thin lips and poured. The tepid, weakly carbonated fluid slid down his throat in a satisfying torrent. His prominent Adam's apple bobbed once, then he set the empty glass back on the bar counter. He brushed the residue of moisture from his pencil mustache with a quick finger, smugly surveying the noisy, happily familiar surroundings.

There was a horseshoe-shaped stand-up bar, dark wood paneling on the walls and the beams overhead; framed sporting prints had been placed strategically around the room. On the service side of the counter, there was a row of upraised beer taps, each emblazoned with the name, the bright crest and colors of a different British brewery. The chalkboard bar-meal menu overhead listed steak and kidney pie, smoked mackerel, toad in the hole. Its only concession to local cuisine was the inevitable paella. Lining Nigel's side of the bar were men in tweeds from Harris and Donegal, men smoking great briar pipes, playing darts, talking football pools.

But for the fact that the innkeeper's name was Juan, and that some of the patrons were dressed in Bermuda shorts and knee socks, Nigel might as well have been back in Birmingham. And that was Spain just the way he liked it: practically wog-less.

A lone, overdressed young woman sitting at one of the low, tiny tables against the wall caught his eye. She gave him a flirtatious smile as she sipped from her gimlet. A shop girl looking for romance.

Nigel cleared his throat and pointedly looked in another direction. That was the other thing he liked about a solo holiday in Spain: all women could be ignored without penalty. For four days and five nights he had no wife to answer to. No secretary. No mistress.

And the pubs didn't close at two-thirty in the afternoon.

He caught the barman's attention with a lifted finger. "Another pint of Theakston's," he said in the colorful accent of his region, rich in the adenoidal, the glottal, as if his sinuses were packed with mushy peas.

The barman smiled knowingly and pointed across the smoke-filled room.

"Uh, what?" Nigel sputtered in confusion, craning his neck to follow the gesture. There was nothing on that side of the room but a sign indicating the direction of the gent's loo. "No, a pint of Theakston's," he insisted, stretching out each syllable and pointing at the requisite tap handle on the other side of the bar.

The bartender shook his head emphatically and with conviction pointed again across the room.

"Bloody flipping wog," Nigel muttered, not entirely under his breath.

"Having some trouble with the natives?" the elderly Briton to Nigel's left asked politely. Pinned to the lapel of his tweed jacket was a paper badge that said "Exe-Tours" and beneath that, in handwritten letters, the name "Alf." "Perhaps I can be of some help?"

Nigel smiled and said, "All I want is another pint of Theakston's."

"No problem that," the old man said, turning away from the bar. He raised a liver-spotted hand. "It's right over there. See the sign above the door?"

Nigel was livid. "Be-ir!" he snarled at the cringing barman. "Be-ir! Any bloody kind of beee-iiir!"

Startled by the outburst, the elderly man took a full step back. "Crikey," he said, "why didn't you say you were French in the first place?"

"Sod off, you old ponce," Nigel growled.

"*Je ne parle*...."

When Nigel raised his clenched fist, the samaritan broke for the lounge. In the tumult Nigel did not see which tap the barman had pulled for him. He eyed the dark-colored liquid in the pint glass suspiciously, but paid up for it.

His first tentative sip told him it was definitely not Theakston's. It tasted like a bitter stout laced with paint thinner. Having already parted with his hard-earned eighty-seven pence, Nigel gritted his teeth and powered it down. "Oh, Lord," he gasped weakly as he shoved the empty glass aside.

The barman clucked his tongue and shook his head. He pointed at the drained glass. "Bishop's Tipple," he said.

"What?" Nigel elbowed the burly man on his right. "Did he say Beeshopstiphole?"

"I hope you're not tryin' to get funny with me, mate. 'Cause if you are, I'm gonna break both your legs."

"No, no, nothing of the kind," Nigel assured him, waving his hands and taking a giant step back. And in so doing he trod on the foot of the man who had moved in behind him.

"Easy, there," the large fellow warned.

"So sorry," Nigel said.

The man, who looked like a lorry driver on holiday, decked out in his Marks and Spencer best, took no offense. "No harm done," he said, peering down at Nigel's empty glass. "Barman, give this gent another of whatever he's drinking.''

''Uh, no . . .'' Nigel began as he saw the bartender reach for the Bishop's Tipple tap.

The large friendly man didn't understand. He thought Nigel was refusing to drink with him. He instantly became a large unfriendly man.

There was nothing to be done. Nigel shut up and watched the dark fluid rush into a fresh pint glass.

''Cheers,'' he said weakly, hoisting the ale to his mouth and taking the tiniest possible sip.

''Cheers,'' the big guy answered, draining his own glass in a single go.

Nigel pulled his hand out of his trouser pocket and put a pound note down on the bar. ''Another,'' he told the bartender, indicating the man's empty glass with a stab of his forefinger.

''Thanks,'' the man told him. ''How about you? Ready for another?''

Nigel looked down at the full pint in his hand and winced. No way could he get another sixteen ounces past his lips. He put the glass back on the bar and said, ''Loo.''

The big man turned and pointed.

''I know, I know,'' Nigel said, shoving away from the bar. He realized at once just how potent the dark brew was. His knees felt oddly springy, not tight-springy but soft-springy. Accordingly, his course across the room did not come close to approximating a straight line.

He pushed open the lavatory door and entered, squinting at the bright light relative to the dim bar. He gave the long, white ceramic urinal a doubtful look. It was the undivided kind, offering no privacy whatsoever, but capable of dealing with as many full bladders as could pack together in front of it. Sheets of water slid constantly down its surface, into a trough below the level of the user's shoes. The idea was to miss the toes of one's own oxfords. As Nigel wasn't confident he could manage that, he stepped into one of the empty toilet stalls instead.

As he reached for his fly there were shouts and screams from the bar. And the sound of breaking glassware.

A fistfight between fans of rival football teams?

Through the rest-room wall it sounded more like a bloody all-out brawl.

His curiosity aroused, his urge to relieve himself stifled, Nigel abandoned the stall and rushed for the lavatory door. He had his hand on the knob when the air was split by the hard crack of a single gunshot. Then another. And another. The shouting took on a frenzied pitch.

Nigel could see three-inch-high headlines in the daily tabloids. Shots fired in holiday pub! Lover's revenge on Majorca! Despite his concern for his own safety, he wanted a peek so badly he could taste it. He proceeded cautiously. He opened the door a scant half inch and put his eye against it.

The urge to relieve himself returned with a vengeance. Unable to help himself, he did so down his trouser leg and into the top of his left shoe.

There were five of them. All dressed in camouflage battle fatigues, dark watch caps, their faces painted green and black. They carried automatic weapons on shoulder slings. Terrorists. I.R.A.? P.L.O.? They didn't bother to identify themselves. They didn't speak at all. They used the metal butts of their assault rifles to herd the patrons away from the bar and back against the wall and the lavatory door.

As the customers moved, Nigel got a glimpse of bodies sprawled on the carpet. Then a man with his back to the door turned suddenly and tried to push his way into the lavatory. Instinctively, Nigel drove his shoulder against the inside of the door, slamming it shut, clicking over the bolt.

He rushed to the sinks in a panic. "Sweet Christ," he moaned aloud. There was a window to the alley but it was barred on the outside.

Then the shooting started in earnest. Not single shots, but a mad barrage of gunfire. Nigel jumped in fright, then clapped his hands over his ears. The terrorists were executing everybody. And even the sustained roar of full-automatic gunfire could not drown out the piercing screams, the shrieks for mercy.

Stray bullets crashed through the lavatory door, shattering the mirror and wall tiles. Nigel threw himself facedown on the floor and crawled for the toilet stalls. The terrible thunder of the shooting actually shook the floor beneath him.

The gunfire ended abruptly. Nigel squirmed into a stall and shut the metal door behind him. He sat on the toilet seat and pulled his legs up, hugging them to his chest, so they wouldn't show under the door. He was suddenly aware of the wetness down his leg and that he was stone-cold sober.

He jerked on the john as the guns barked again, single shots and short bursts.

Coups de grace.

Don't let them come in here! he prayed. Dear God, don't let them come in!

A hobnailed boot slammed against the door. Once, twice. The door splintered and gave on the third kick, banging back against the wall.

Nigel shut his eyes tight. He thought the terrorists would check each of the four closed stalls for victims in hiding. He anticipated having to listen to each door squeak open in turn until they came to his. He was wrong.

There was an easier, quicker way to dispense with any stragglers. Autofire roared deafeningly in the tiny, tiled room. Bullets stitched across the metal doors of all four stalls at navel height. Nigel saw the jagged holes appear in the door in front of him at the same instant he felt the terrible pain in his legs and chest. Reflexively, he squeezed his knees tighter to his torso, staring down in horror at the blood pouring from his ruined stomach. It rushed down over his crotch, dripping and splattering into the toilet bowl.

"Help me," Nigel gasped as the water under him turned pink, then quickly red. He knew he was dying; he didn't know how fast. He managed one more agonized breath before he did the dance.

16

Billy Two raced down the middle of the dark, winding road. His bare feet made no sound, no telltale slap of flesh on asphalt; he ran on the balls of his feet and his toes. The prickling in his skin had not eased with the removal of his clothes; it had gotten worse. The garments had, in fact, been acting as a kind of buffer, protecting him from his own heightened perceptions. Naked, he could sense every rock, every tree for a distance of twenty feet in all directions; he could feel their shapes, feel the objects pushing back at him as he sprinted past. It was as if his whole skin was acting as an echo locater. He could have shut his eyes and still found his way along the sharply curving track.

It was madness.

Some tiny part of him knew it, too.

Knew the feeling of limitless power, of impossible abilities, was the result of mental overload, of prolonged psychotropic drug therapy and its sudden withdrawal, of his own long repressed, compressed fury at being treated like a fucking lab animal. The surviving rational bit of him was only along for the ride, however; it had no power, except to observe. What it observed was William Starfoot II lost in his own obscure Amerind wonderland.

For as long as he could remember, Billy Two had wanted to return to the purity of the time before the coming of the white man, to his ancestral birthright: the primeval forest and the intimate, sacred contact between the living creatures and inanimate things that populated it. He had always longed to be truly one with the world—and now, he was literally that. He was a conscious part of the seething molecular whole.

It was not wonderland as he had imagined it; there was no serenity, no peace, only rage and an overpowering urge to release it. The urge to kill.

Sharp stones gouged the soles of his feet as he ran, but he felt no pain. He had acquired the power to shut out the nonessential, the distractions; only one thing mattered, reaching Ca'n Hatton. He slowed his pace as he approached the bottom of the winding stretch of pavement and the long straightaway that preceded the roadblock.

On either side of the lane, crude stone fences had been piled three feet high. He climbed over the one on the left and continued on, padding through dewy grass and leaves in the failing purple light. Every step he took brought him closer to the flashing blue beacon. When he was within fifteen feet he dropped to his belly and crawled. He stopped when he was directly across from the police car.

He did not think about what he was going to do next. He was operating on automatic, on instinct, intuition. And his intuition told him that his life, for the time being at least, was charmed, protected, that his enemies could do nothing to hurt him, that he was free to collect all that was owed.

Billy Two vaulted the wall, dropping silently to the other side. He landed in a crouch, then sprang at once onto the rear trunk lid of the police car.

The Spetsnaz soldier leaning against the back fender was dressed for his role. He had the proper dark green uniform, the Sam Brown belt, the 9mm Star submachine gun; he even had the odd, black, inverted flowerpot-shaped hat of a *guardia*. But the obscenity that burst from his throat as the naked brown man leaped past his nose was straight from downtown Leningrad.

Billy Two cut the curse off short, jamming the muzzle of the Makarov in his left hand between the stunned trooper's parted lips and teeth. At the same instant, he pulled the trigger. The autopistol cracked and a rain of ComBloc brains pelted the tarmac.

The Indian did not pause. There was another armed imposter to be dealt with. He jumped to the roof of the cop car, straddling the flashing light. Billy thrust the gun in his right hand down, probing with his mind, feeling through the metal roof for the epicenter of the Spetsnaz soldier's cranium. Before he located it, a thunderous roar erupted from beneath his feet. Slugs ripped up through the roof of the car, howling past his face and into the darkening sky. Billy fired once, throwing the switch that shut off the shooting from below.

He hopped onto the car's hood, bending down, peering through the front windshield. In the ghastly green light of the instrument panel the driver was definitely dead: his right eye looked east, his left eye stared due south, his chin was nowhere in sight.

Billy jumped to the ground, crossed the road, then climbed over the stone wall on the other side. As he crab-crawled behind it, parallel to the road, in the direction of Ca'n Hatton, he heard the sounds of men moving quickly toward him on the pavement, heading for the cop car. He counted feet. Three pairs. In crepe soles.

He let them come within fifteen feet, then rose from belly to knees to feet, popping up from behind the wall with the two Makarovs leveled chest high. The three men, all in nightfighter black, their faces smeared with camo war paint, ran right under his guns. It all happened so fast they couldn't even slow down, let alone get their AKs pointed the right way. Billy Two rapid-fired with both hands as they dashed past, the twin strobe-light muzzle-flashes freeze-framing grimaces of surprise and pain. He turned with his targets, tracking them, the compact handguns bucking frantically in his fists. The hail of 9mm slugs twisted the soldiers of Spetsnaz sideways and down, slamming them to the asphalt.

Then all fourteen rounds were spent; the strobe lights winked out. The hillsides echoed and reechoed the tight string of reports. From the dark road there were soft, desperate groans. Billy Two dropped the empty weapons behind the wall and ran.

The sky above him was starless, moonless, and his lean brown body practically invisible, a shadow sliding over a sea of ink. He ran another 100 yards, until he came to the corner of the steeply sloping field. He jumped the perpendicular wall, onto the grounds of Ca'n Hatton, then turned uphill into the maze of the almond groves. The trees hadn't been planted in evenly spaced rows; they were staggered irregularly, following the shapes of the terraces, which conformed to the rounded contours of the hillside. Accordingly, with the trees in full bloom, even in full daylight, it was impossible to see far into the groves. It was also impossible to walk for more than a few yards without having to skirt a tree.

Billy climbed quickly but with care, easing the obstructing branches out of his way. When he came to the six-yard-high stone wall that buttressed the next higher terrace level, he turned left, following the moss-draped barrier toward its intersection with the *estancia*'s zigzagging access road.

When he was within spitting distance of the road's second hairpin, he stopped and listened. He was not alone. He heard voices speaking in whispers. Speaking Russian.

Billy Two climbed the terrace wall, finding finger and footholds in the gaps in the ancient mortar. He walked parallel to the top of the wall, keeping behind the line of trees until he was right above the hairpin. Then he stepped out from behind the screen of branches and trunks.

Below him, on the downhill inside part of the turn, were four Spetsnaz troopers in blacksuits. They were crouched, assault rifles at the ready, waiting for the radio signal to advance and engage. The brief flurry of gunfire from the direction of the roadblock had them shifting around anxiously, raring to go. They knew in all likelihood first blood had already been drawn. Their mission's hourglass had been inverted and the numbers were falling fast.

Starfoot left the troopers to their prebattle jitters and stepped back into the line of trees. He walked alongside and above the road until he was sixty feet from the next hairpin, then he slipped down the terrace wall and onto the road. The angle of the narrow lane to the slope and the assymetrical placement of the terraces made a detour necessary. Unless he wanted to walk the road, which he didn't, he had to go down again before he could go up.

He crossed the pavement and climbed down the supporting wall on the downslope side. He continued in the direction he had been traveling for another thirty yards, until he was well past the hairpin, then turned ninety degrees right. He scaled the terrace wall, heading straight uphill for the bunkhouse and, farther on, farther up, the estate's main building.

Billy Two moved quickly, silently, through the obstacle course of almond trees. As he rounded the side of one tree, intent on making time, he almost walked on the heels of a Spetsnaz soldier moving ahead of him.

Almost.

With catlike body control Billy Two froze instantly in place.

The trooper heard nothing to his back. He did not stop or turn. By the time he took another two steps, circling the tree trunk, the Indian was no longer behind him.

Starfoot had turned the other way, doubling back on his own tracks. When he headed upslope again, he did so at an angle to the estimated path of the trooper. Almost at once, from his left, one tree over, came the sound of a man moving right in step with him. Billy had penetrated the wedge formation of an advancing Spetsnaz fireteam. He had to get in front of it, in front of the team leader on point. And the only way to do that was to slow it down.

Screams.

What he needed were screams.

He cut farther to his left, rounding a tree, timing his move so once again he came up behind an oblivious Soviet trooper, the last man in line on that side of the wedge. The soldier in black was a full eight inches shorter than Billy, but their weights were roughly the same, in the neighborhood of two hundred pounds. The trooper had an AK-74, full Kevlar-type body armor, a day pack and a battle harness heavy with dangling grenades.

Starfoot never saw his face.

He tripped the man from behind, sending him crashing to the ground. The trooper tried to roll on impact, but Billy was already diving on top of him, driving a shoulder into his kidneys, knocking the air from his lungs. Before the man could recover, cry out or start to fight back, the Indian shifted his position. He planted his bare butt on the small of the soldier's back, then lunged forward and grabbed hold of the man's right foot, hauling it back against his own chest. With the heel of the trooper's shoe in his left hand, the toe in his right, Billy Two gave a vicious clockwise twist, snapping the anklebone like a bread stick.

A bellow of pain erupted from beneath him.

Then Billy did the same to the other foot. He did it quickly, cleanly, despite the frantic thrashing of the pinned man.

The screaming more than doubled in volume.

It was enough to momentarily stop the fire-team's advance, to bring troopers to their comrade's aid on the double.

Before that could happen, Starfoot darted away, circling wide to avoid further contact. When he was certain he was clear, he sprinted uphill, through the almond-tree obstacle course. The injured trooper was still screaming as Billy scrambled up the retaining wall that stood between himself and the bunkhouse level.

The bunkhouse stood no more than fifteen feet from the edge of the terrace. A converted cow shed, it had been modernized around the turn of the century. It had the same thick, mortared stone walls as the main house but its tile roof had been replaced with sheets of corrugated metal. The row of tiny, unevenly spaced windows on the valley side of the building were shuttered and dark. What feeble light there was came from the main house on the terrace above and was filtered through a dense screen of tree limbs.

Billy Two slipped silently along the side of the bunkhouse, rounding the rear right corner. As he turned, he came face to face with a dark-skinned, curly-haired man in a T-shirt. A T-shirt stretched almost to bursting by a massively muscled torso. The curly-haired man held an AR-16 in two hands, its butt braced against his hip, its flash-hider muzzle locked on the center of Billy Two's chest.

They stood frozen in place for a long moment.

As the muscle man sized up the naked brown intruder, his tight, deadly expression melted away. It was replaced by a look of pure astonishment.

Billy Two broke the impasse. "Don't be coy, Alex. We both know goddamn well you're going to say it. So go ahead. Get it the hell over with."

The Greek lowered his weapon, an enormous grin spreading over his mug.

"Hole-eee shit!" he howled.

17

The sound of autofire clattering up the valley set Barrabas's pulse racing. It was the beginning of the end. And he was damned glad of it. For the first time in weeks, he was free to stop thinking, stop worrying, to put aside the impossible odds he and his SOBs faced, to start doing something about whittling them down.

He sat crouched against the lowermost terrace wall, his back pressed into a deep concavity in the stonework, a dull black, Parkerized finish commando knife in his extended right hand. He was part of the wall. Invisible. Barely breathing. His eyes, his ears, strained to pick up the slightest hint of movement in front of him.

On this mission, as far as the assignments went, nobody had drawn a pass. There were no free rides with so few to defend against an uncounted force of attackers. Every point Barrabas had decided to fortify would take heavy heat; that was guaranteed. He had left the most difficult task for himself and Liam O'Toole. That was to penetrate the enemy advance, to harass, to inflict as many casualties as possible, to do it on the run. Free-lance. It was the kind of job both Barrabas and O'Toole liked.

Hardnose.

A twig snapped off to his left.

Spetsnaz was infiltrating the lowest terrace.

Barrabas did not move. He had confidence in his position. He knew damned well that even if the GRU boys were equipped with electronic eyes-in-the-night, they couldn't see through things. Things like tree trunks, limbs, branches heavy with blossom.

He strained even harder to hear, to gauge the speed and angle of the enemy advance. To his left. At least five of them. They were definitely all to his left. And not more than ten yards away. In the almond groves, ten yards might as well have been a hundred. Line of sight was less than two. The soft rustling grew louder, then stopped. The Spetsnaz soldiers were rendez-vousing, reforming at the wall.

Barrabas could not see them, but he could anticipate exactly what they were going to do. One at a time, they would climb the wall. Then, when they were all up, assuming they met no immediate hard resistance, they would regroup into their traveling formation and continue on to the next obstacle. That gave him both the time and the opportunity to inflict some damage.

The white-haired man eased out of the depression in the wall and advanced, heading for the source of the sounds. He kept the wall on his right shoulder, moving quickly but with extreme care. A snapped twig under his foot would mean discovery, a lost opportunity on his part and possible pursuit by a superior force.

As he approached, he could hear the soldiers climbing the wall, one by one. He could hear their breathing, the soft rustle of their gear, the occasional scrape of their boots against the stones. And when the scraping sounds stopped, there was a quick, low whistle, barely audible. The signal for the next man to start up.

Barrabas had to risk moving closer to count heads. He leaned into the tree in front of him, pushing a branch up ever so slightly. He saw two dark shapes, men dressed in black kneeling at the foot of the wall, waiting their turn to join the others. The low whistle came from above and the man farthest away from him began to climb.

Barrabas did not wait for the climber to reach the top of the roughly ten-foot-high barrier. He advanced at once, slipping up behind the remaining trooper who still knelt on the ground. He struck with precision that came from long practice, using both hands. He reached across the man's forehead with his left, digging his fingers into the right temple; he reached in front of the man's throat with his right hand, pressing the point of the knife just under the trooper's left ear. There was no pause in the motion; it was all one, all fluid, smooth. Barrabas jerked the soldier's head hard to the left at the same moment he slashed left to right, drawing the full length of the dagger's blade across, around the exposed throat. The razor-sharp steel made a quick, ripping sound as it opened the trooper's neck from ear to ear.

Barrabas really put some power into the slash stroke, enough to cut cleanly through windpipe and voice box. There would be no cry for help. Blood from severed jugular and carotid hissed, spurting over his right hand and forearm, bathing his fingers in sticky warmth. He clamped his arms around the dying man's shoulders, hugging the quivering body tight to him for a seemingly endless fifteen seconds, until the thrashing ended.

One down.

As he leaned the new-made corpse forward on its face, the low whistle came again from above. It was a summons no one was going to answer.

Barrabas stepped over the body and away from the wall. It wouldn't be long before the Spetsnaz fireteam reacted, returned for their missing member. He didn't know precisely how they would organize the backtrack down the wall, but he knew they would do it en masse, clean and by the numbers. They would also do it very carefully.

As he put distance between himself and the dead man's pals, he thought he heard a second low whistle behind and above him. He knew there wouldn't be another one; the rest of them would be coming.

He had his next hiding spot along the wall already picked out, the route to it memorized. After taking only a half-dozen more steps, he knew he wasn't going to make it.

Another advancing fireteam.

Dead ahead.

Between him and his sanctuary.

He stopped and knelt down beside the wall. He had a choice. He could sit tight and hope that the two attack units weren't in radio contact, that the one in front of him hit the barrier in a hurry and got the hell out of his way, that the team he had just hit didn't decide to work toward him looking to revenge their man. If the two fireteams tried to link up with him in the middle, his ass was going to be in a sling, but quick. The alternative was for him to go over the wall himself and abandon his mission.

One second Barrabas had a choice, the next it was out of his hands.

A Spetsnaz trooper appeared out of nowhere. He had night-sight goggles on his head. Not that he needed them. As he rounded the trunk of a tree on the run, he practically fell over Barrabas.

There was no time for anything neat or cute.

Barrabas reacted like a rattlesnake, striking instinctively. He lunged forward with the knife

in front of him. The trooper tried to deflect the
point of the blade with the butt of his AK. Barrabas beat him, thrusting the dagger through
the front of his body armor, but he didn't make
the stab where he wanted to. It was low and to the
left. Through the stomach instead of the heart.

The force of the stab lunge turned and
slammed the soldier back into the wall. His AK
fell from his hands.

Barrabas rode the man around, lifting up on
the knife handle as he did so, trying to saw up
with the double-edged blade to center chest and
a fast kill. The body armor refused to give. The
knife remained in place, even though Barrabas
raised the man up on tiptoe.

Then the trooper started to yell. Barrabas
clamped a hand over his mouth. And hauled the
dagger out. The blade, diamond-shaped in cross
section, left a wound track that would not close.
Pulling it out was like unplugging a drain in a
slaughterhouse. Gore sprayed Barrabas's shirtfront and fatigues. He stabbed again, this time
plunging the dagger point under the trooper's
chin. He drove the knife in to the hilt, in and up,
sending seven inches of Sheffield's best sliding
straight into his head, the last inch and a half
skewering his brain.

Two down.

The sounds of running feet came at Barrabas
from all directions. He let the man slump to the
ground and, without trying to pull out the deep-

ly embedded knife, scrambled up the wall and over.

The pursuit was right on his tail, no longer making any attempt at stealth, crashing through the tree branches. He hauled his Browning Hi-Power from hip leather, cycling the action, putting a live round under the hammer, as he dashed ahead of the footfalls.

From the other side of the estate there came a terrible shrill and quavering cry of agony. Then another, even louder, even more frantic.

Barrabas had only one thought: he hoped to hell it was a Commie in pain.

LIAM O'TOOLE HEARD the wail, as well.

For him, it couldn't have come at a worse time.

The source of the noise was behind him, from over his shoulder. It was also to the back of the Spetsnaz trooper he was creeping up on.

The trooper pivoted with his AK-74, turning by reflex toward the sound, and found himself staring down into the glaring eyes of a short, broadly built man in blackface who stood not four feet away. Even as the soldier swung the muzzle of his assault rifle around, trying to lock it on the target's chest, the short man was no longer standing; he was jumping to the side.

O'Toole had a stiletto in his right hand and a silenced Beretta 92SB in his left. He had intended to get in close so he could use the knife. That was out of the question now.

So, as he ducked away from the sights of the AK, he raised his left hand and fired.

The range was approximately three and a half feet.

In the bright yellow light of the muzzle-flash, O'Toole saw the hole appear above the bridge of the trooper's nose. A small black hole. The man's head snapped back as his brainpan emptied and then the light winked out. The afterimage of death grimace burned into his retina, O'Toole heard the corpse thud to earth in front of him.

So did just about everybody else.

"Misha?" said a whispered voice very close.

Too goddamn close.

Liam needed some room to operate. It was time for the O'Toole turkey call.

"Uhhhhh," he answered softly, sheathing his commando dagger, taking a two-handed grip on the Beretta as he squatted down beside the dead man.

His fellow trooper was not the birdbrain Liam had hoped. Instead of charging in headfirst, he charged in AK first. With the night-vision goggles he easily picked up two bodies where there should only have been one. His target sighted, he let rip. A yard of flame belched from the muzzle of his rifle. From straight on it appeared as a bright yellow point surrounded by a gas cloud of incandescent orange.

Steel-cored slugs slammed into the wall behind O'Toole's head, showering him with stinging fragments. He dropped to his belly. If the Spetsnaz trooper hadn't been firing on the run, Liam wouldn't have had a chance. But as it was, he managed to return fire. He aimed for a point just above the yellow spot that marked the AK's muzzle, then squeezed the trigger as fast as he could, raising his sights with each successive shot, walking the 9mm hollowpoint slugs up the trooper's torso. The Beretta's seven muffled reports were inaudible over the mad clatter of the Kalashnikov on full-auto. Their effect, however, was both immediate and devastating.

The first three bullets hit body armor. The fourth hit throat. The fifth chin. The sixth teeth. And the last pushed aside the trooper's left eyeball and tracked straight through his head.

The dead man collapsed to his back, arms flung overhead, his hand convulsing around the AK's pistol grip, his corpse finger pinning down the trigger. The AK continued to bark and flash, spraying the grove's downslope with the final fifteen rounds in its magazine.

Before the mag emptied, O'Toole was on the move. He headed back the way he had come, back toward the access road at a brisk trot.

He ran with confidence, sure of every step, every turn. Spetsnaz had certainly underestimated the difficulty of the terrain. Night goggles or not, they would've improved their odds by attacking by day. It was a question of the right equipment in the wrong place.

Against the wrong people.

Liam kidded himself about a lot of things, but he always took the basics of his profession seriously. He knew the lives he and Barrabas were taking wouldn't, couldn't alter the night's ultimate outcome. No matter how well they knew the ground, how good they were at down-and-dirty fighting, they could not kill enough of the enemy to make a difference.

It was a matter of mathematics.

Of simple logic.

No amount of which would make the SOBs go down quietly. They had far too much pride for that.

Logic had nothing to do with O'Toole's immediate dislike of the colonel's plan for a retreat and last-ditch defense of the casa, either. He flat out despised retreats and last stands. Both were an admission of defeat. As far as he was concerned, it wasn't over until it was over. If he had been the commander, Liam undoubtedly would have staged a breakout over the mountains. Breakout and scatter. By dawn Spetsnaz's numbers would have run out.

This time.

O'Toole scowled as he ducked under a branch. Yeah, that was the big problem and he damn well knew it. If some or all of the SOBs got away, it wouldn't have put an end to anything, only postponed the inevitable, given the unlimited resources available to Spetsnaz. The inevitable was more pursuit. More attacks. And the eventual destruction, even if it was one by one, of the whole team. Maybe it was better to go out in a final blaze of C-4-powered glory.

Maybe.

O'Toole was a demolitions expert who preferred to do his killing face-to-face. A brief stint in the I.R.A. as a teenager had taught him to hate bombs and terrorists. Both were too indiscriminate as to their targets. And both often missed the target altogether.

There was no getting around the fact that every mission the SOBs had drawn had been a certified no-win. And that Barrabas had always managed to pull their butts out of the fire. Tonight's bit of magic was going to be a dilly, one way or another.

O'Toole slowed his pace as he neared the road. He approached the inside of the third hairpin, just back from the top of the wall. The closer he got to the turn, the lower the wall became and the scarcer the cover. He crawled the last bit, peering over a mound of soft, damp moss.

He saw nothing on the road opposite. He inched farther forward until he could see over the wall and directly below him. He nearly soiled his pants. Not two feet from the tip of his nose four troopers lay prone on the road in the lee of the hairpin, waiting for a signal to move on.

Liam moved carefully away from the edge, rolling to his back. He couldn't get all four with the Beretta, not with piss-poor light and them wearing body armor. He put the handgun back into its webbed shoulder holster and pulled an M-67 frag grenade from his battle harness. He eased out the safety clip, then, holding down the safety lever, pulled the pin.

O'Toole took a slow breath and let it slide out. Then he opened his hand slightly, making the safety lever flip off against his chest, silently. He counted to one, raising his hand over his head, over the edge of the wall, over the road and the troopers. He counted to two. On three, he let the grenade drop. As he did so, he rolled forward, away from the road, curling and covering.

The fuse was set for a bona fide four-second delay.

No sooner had he got his arms over his head, than the night was ripped by an ear-splitting, ground-shaking whump! If there were screams, the sound of the explosion buried them. O'Toole escaped all the other blast effects, shielded by the stone wall that turned most of the whump out and up into the troopers.

Then it was raining bits and pieces.

Liam jumped to his feet and started uphill as fast as his legs would carry him.

There was a shout to his back. Then autofire. Slugs whining over his head, slashing through the trees all around him. That's precisely what he hated about bombs. Sometimes they didn't get the whole job done.

There was more than bullets coming after him; there was the tramp of feet as well.

"Fucking A!" Liam said, yanking another M-67 off his harness, arming it and letting it drop behind him without waiting for it to cook. It could damn well cook while he sprinted.

Behind him the grove rocked with another bomb.

The shooting not only continued, it got better.

A freight train hit the back of Liam's right shoulder and he went down hard on his face.

18

Sergeant Ilin watched the pale-green ghost figures shift about behind a waist-high screen of limestone boulder. She lowered her Starlite scope and said, "If there are more than two of them guarding the summit, they are much better soldiers than Captain Balandin gave them credit for."

Her unit had been in position to take the peak overlooking Ca'n Hatton for more than an hour. They had been listening with keen interest to the goings-on in the valley and to the flurries of coded chatter pingponging back and forth over the Spetsnaz communications system. When the sporadic bursts of small-arms fire and screams first began, Ilin and her team thought a mistake had been made, that the downhill units had attacked prematurely, before the signal from command. From the radio talk it became clear that there had been no mistake, that the ruckus had been caused by the cornered mercenaries who were fighting back, hit-and-run style, as the fireteams advanced.

Fighting back to some effect, if confusion and consternation was their intent.

"How could they be so stupid?" one of the corporals said as he scanned the summit outpost with his own Starlite scope. "How could they possibly leave their most vulnerable point so weakly defended?"

"It's not a matter of choice on their part," Ilin said, smiling. "It's a matter of manpower. They don't have enough to adequately cover any part of their perimeter."

"What are we waiting for then?"

The corporal's question was on all their minds. Ilin's included. Two mercenaries, no matter how well armed, could not possibly hold them off for long. Ilin sympathized with her men's urge to get into the fray. They had hauled not only their own standard-issue, individual assault gear up the backbreaking and treacherous cliffs, but also four rocket-propelled grenade launchers and dozens of rounds each of additional HE rockets. They were understandably anxious to see the damnable things put to use.

Ilin could answer the question about the cause for the delay.

It was Balandin.

All Balandin.

For any number of reasons the egotistical bastard wanted to be there, directing the finish of the operation. For one thing, he wanted to revenge himself, personally, upon the woman who had yanked his balls off. The sergeant smiled. As far as she was concerned it couldn't have happened to a more deserving fellow. Under different circumstances, she might have even enjoyed a conversation with the female SOB, if only to get the gory details of Balandin's emasculation.

There was more at stake than just the honor of captain and corps. Balandin not only wanted to raise Spetsnaz's colors from the dung heap, but his own as well. He wanted all the credit for a successful retaliation mission. Only that would allow him to regain the face he had lost with his superiors after the Tarkotovo disaster.

The trek up the mountain from the beach hadn't been that hard on Sergeant Ilin. In her Olympic-grade physical condition, for her it was only a moderate workout. Still the sergeant hadn't enjoyed the hike. She knew she had pulled the assignment because the captain hated her as much as she hated him. He had handed her the roughest job of all because he knew she'd die before she'd give him the satisfaction of seeing her fail. Because she was a competitor, a winner. It was the knowledge that she was being manipulated by a man she despised that made the morning's outing laborious, not the mountain.

Now that she was in position she was glad she had stuck with it. The key to the success of the whole mission was in her most capable hands. She would be the one to take the high ground. And from the summit, firing their RPGs straight down, her men could literally blow the Hatton casa apart, stone by stone. They would do the same to the Soldiers of Barrabas. Or they would drive the mercenary scum from the cover of the disintegrating building and into the sights of the troopers waiting below.

When the honors were passed out, Sergeant Ilin was sure to get her share, no matter how Captain Balandin choreographed the finale.

A different kind of noise boomed up at them.

It echoed from the valley walls.

"Grenade," the corporal said.

"One of theirs," Ilin said. She raised the Starlite scope, putting the rubber eyecup to her eye and squinting into the lens. The slight movement on top of the summit had ceased. The defenders were no longer anywhere in sight. Perhaps they had finally settled in to make their stand? Perhaps they had finally seen the futility of the battle and had abandoned the position altogether?

Another explosion boomed up from below.

Another one of theirs.

Soon, Sergeant Ilin told herself as she continued to scan the rock line for head shapes. Soon all the questions would be answered.

And the corpses counted.

BALANDIN STOOD some distance away from his command car, listening to the relayed situation reports as the fireteams called in, according to schedule or need. Things were going pretty much as the captain had anticipated, though the SOBs had inflicted more and quicker damage to his troops than expected. The loss of five men at the sham *guardia* roadblock was particularly perplexing to him as he had been certain that he had containment on all the mercenaries. The prospect that he hadn't was what made him stand apart from and not sit in his car. It was too easy a target.

Then the grenade exploded on the slope above them. They could actually see the burst of light through the lacy veil of tree limb and blossom.

"Damn!" Balandin exclaimed. "Who got it?"

Lieutenant Skorokhvatov lowered his headset. "Team Beta," he said. "Just as they were preparing to go around the third hairpin."

"How many hurt?"

"Two dead, one wounded," the lieutenant answered. Again he pressed one of the headset's phones to his ear for a moment, then said, "The surviving troopers from Beta are in pursuit of the ambusher. They have him in sight. And they have been joined by fireteam Alpha."

At least one of the bastards wasn't going to get away, Balandin thought.

The second grenade explosion made him wince.

"Well?" he demanded of Skorokhvatov.

The lieutenant gave him a helpless gesture.

There was nothing he could do until the casualty report came in. When it did he had reason to smile. "Good news, sir," he said, "no injuries from the second grenade."

"Have they got him?"

Skorokhvatov conferred with the men on the other end of the radio link. His smile faded. "No, not yet," he reported, "but they have him completely surrounded and he has been wounded. They are certain of that."

"Are the other units in position?"

The lieutenant referred to a check sheet, before responding in the affirmative. "Yes, sir, we're ready to begin the attack at your command."

Balandin scowled up at the hillside. In one respect the operation was already proving a major disappointment to him. He had fantasized long and hard over this moment; he had fully expected the pleasure of having his quarry squirm and squeal in the noose of steel he held them in.

There was no squirming.

And the only squealing so far had come from dying and wounded troopers of Spetsnaz.

If the SOBs were pissing their pants in the face of their own certain destruction, they had a very unsatisfactory way of showing it.

There was no point in postponing the assault any longer.

"Give them the attack signal," Balandin said. "And have my squad ready to move. I want to be on the scene as soon as the main building is surrounded.''

Skorokhvatov spoke into the mouthpiece.

And suddenly the hills were alive with auto-fire.

19

Claude Hayes peered out from between a cleft in the crumbling limestone bedrock, looking over the sights and flash-hider of his M16A1.

"See anything?" Dr. Lee asked from the darkness to his back.

The two of them had taken cover behind the ring of boulders atop the ridge peak they had been assigned to defend.

"A whole lot of nothing," Hayes said, pulling back and dropping to his butt on the ground. He held his rifle across his chest, his right hand wrapped around the pistol grip, his left twisted through the sling strap and holding the hand guard. The M-16 was set for automatic fire and the safety had been off for the past three hours, ever since he and the lady doctor had gotten into position. "I know they're out there," he muttered. "I can hear 'em breathing."

"You and me both," Dr. Lee said. "I feel like a fly about to get swatted."

It felt even worse than that to Hayes.

As if the two of them were alone at the very

top of the world, which also just happened to be ground zero at a nuclear test site. It felt worse, but Hayes kept his mouth shut.

Offhand, he couldn't think of anyone he'd rather die beside than Dr. Leona Hatton. He also couldn't think of anyone that he would less like to see die than the slim, black-haired woman. In the months that they had shared the endless work on her rambling wreck of an estate, he had become closer to her than to any of the other SOBs.

It was more than just the isolation.

And it sure as hell wasn't sex because that was one thing they didn't share, by mutual agreement. Sex invariably screwed up a good friendship.

Hayes and Hatton, despite their widely differing backgrounds, were a lot alike. They were both loners. Individualists. Less interested in the joys of the flesh and the grape than the other mercenaries, they could be quiet, introspective. And they needed their privacy.

They were attracted to the SOBs by more than money. The missions allowed otherwise hidden and contradictory parts of their natures to surface. Allowed the physician's healing hand to turn to a fist. Allowed the seeker-of-peace-within to study war. All in the name of justice.

"There they go again," Dr. Lee said, as the autofire clattered from below.

"Any time now," Hayes told her, "we can expect to get some company."

They were as ready as they could be. They had their extra 40-round mags lined up within easy reach. Frag grenades, too, in neat rows in the dirt.

When they took their first enemy salvo, they both realized how pathetic their preparations had been. Rocket-propelled grenades screamed up at them from the opposing peaks, triangulating on their position, and the world turned into a horror dream of deafening concussions, of shuddering earth, of exploding rock and metal. For interminable seconds it was all they could do to hang on to the ground.

Then, as suddenly as it had begun, the barrage stopped. And the blinding HE klieg lights winked out. Rocks, ranging from softball size down to pebbles, rained down on them amid the choking pall of cordite smoke and limestone dust.

Both Hayes and Hatton knew what was coming next. Suitably softened up by RPGs, they were about to be overrun by Russia's finest. The SOBs already had their game plan down.

There were only two marginally secure paths to the summit. The one they had used to get up, which began at the back of the main building, and one that came from the opposite direction, the direction of the sea. They weren't worried about Spetsnaz circling the peak and coming up behind them on the casa path. In fact, they hoped the troopers tried it because it was certain death, even in daylight.

The other way was a different story.

It followed the curve of a jagged semicircular cliff, then angled up through a jumble of Volkswagen-size boulders. It offered excellent protection for the attackers until they got within a hundred feet or so of the summit. After that, it was Sprint City. If the troopers weren't already at the end of the boulder line, ready to make the mad rush, they would be moving to it in short order, before the memory of the rocket-grenade attack dimmed.

If the Spetsnaz soldiers were worried about Hayes and Hatton regaining their courage, they had nothing to worry about. The two SOBs had never lost it.

Before the dust had cleared and rocks had stopped falling, both Claude and Dr. Lee were up and at 'em. Hayes had spent the last hours of light setting up his aiming stakes. The effort paid off now. He slithered around a boulder, laid his M-16's barrel in the deeply notched stick and even in the swirling dust and dark, when he pinned the trigger, ripping off a neat 10-round burst, he knew his cone of fire was on target, that its beaten zone encircled the last point of cover for the enemy.

The assault rifle bucked against his shoulder again as he sprayed a dozen more 5.56mm tumblers downhill. The ricochets whined off the cliff face.

"Give it to 'em, Claude!" Dr. Lee said. "Let 'em know we're still here!"

The black man emptied his rifle in a long burst, then rolled away. Dr. Lee rolled right into the spot he had left, thrusting her M-16 into the same notch, snugging the butt of the stock to her shoulder and cutting loose.

Spent brass plinked against the stones as she poured lead onto the still invisible enemy. She fired shorter bursts than Hayes because they were easier for her to control. When she came up empty, the black man was reloaded and ready to rock and roll some more. As they switched positions something whooshed over the rock in front of them, over the tops of their heads by no more than two feet. The shock wave of its passing blasted grit into their faces.

"Sweet Lord," Hayes groaned as the RPG howled on over the peak.

"Shooting star," Dr. Lee said, turning to follow the track of the rocket.

It self-destructed with a brilliant flash high over the valley.

"My kind of fireworks," Hayes said.

All joking aside, they both knew they were damned lucky. The rocket-propelled grenades followed a draftsman's line track from point of launch to point of impact. No trajectory. Because their attackers were below them and using RPGs, they couldn't lob a bomb into the laps of Hayes and Hatton.

They could, however, ram one straight up their respective noses.

Not easily intimidated, even by HE projectiles traveling a thousand feet per second, Claude dropped into position in front of the aiming stake. The smoke and dust had filtered away. He could not see Spetsnaz, but he could see the pretty lights they made.

Yellow flashes among the rocks.

And a staccato chattering.

Steel-jacketed lead flailed the boulders all around him. He covered his eyes with his hand to protect them from flying rock chips. He covered his eyes, but he shot back. He didn't need eyes to find the beaten zone. All he needed was a finger to pull the trigger.

"Are they coming?" Lee yelled at him, flat on her back below the protection of the boulders.

"Doc, how the hell should I know?" Hayes yelled back over the full-auto clatter he was making and the multiple full-auto pounding their position was taking.

"Time for a wake-up call," she said, picking up a frag grenade. She primed it and chucked it over the boulder, sending it sailing downhill without waiting for the fuse to burn down. Five seconds later the air was ripped by a flat crump! There was a hesitation, a low bass rumble, then a whole shelf of rotten rock somewhere along the cliff face gave way, thundering down into the saddle between the peaks.

"Jesus! Did you aim that thing or what?" Hayes said.

"Or what," Lee admitted.

The rock slide caused a momentary lull in the small-weapons fire poured on their position.

"Bad news," Hayes told her as the AKs raked the hilltop with slugs. "Here they come."

He ducked back just in time to avoid being caught in the enemy beaten zone. The insane concentration of lead chewed the ground to powder and his aiming stake to toothpicks.

"Wake-up calls all around," Lee said, yanking the double safeties of the frag grenade, letting the handle plink off, then throwing it. Her hand went right to another grenade.

Claude started doing the same thing.

The grenades exploded downslope in an erratic string. There were no more landslides, however. And the AKs kept right on firing, pinning them down.

"We've got to go for it," Lee said, counting her last three grenades. "You know they're just going to lay flat down there until we run out of firecrackers. We've got to hit them with some bullets."

"Right," Hayes said. "On two...one...."

"Two!" Lee shouted, her M-16 tight to her shoulder.

As she popped up from behind a boulder, the enemy fire stopped.

They were coming all right.

They had been coming for quite a while, too.

The supporting fire had stopped so it

wouldn't hit the charging men in the back. They were that close.

Lee punched a triplet of hot tumblers into the center of an onrushing trooper's chest. Three puffs of dust. And the soldier didn't even slow down. He had a hand grenade clutched in his right fist.

"Armor!" she barked at Hayes as she corrected her point of aim. "Head shots! Take head shots!" She swept her sights across the man's face as she pinned the trigger. Multiple hit.

The back of his skull exploded in a puff of pink mist and he fell forward, suddenly limp, to the rocks less than five feet from where she lay.

The grenade rolled out of his lifeless hand, its safety lever popping free.

"Cover!" she shouted, burying her face in the dirt.

The rocking boom deposited a good pound of soil on the back of her head.

Coughing, spitting, Lee swung on a new target, a man vaulting the boulders to her left, vaulting and firing his AK at the same time. He should have done either one or the other. She slammed a 2-round volley into the side of his head. His legs crumpled as he hit the dirt, AK flying off into the dark, end over end.

Hayes knelt behind the line of boulders, ignoring the possibility of catching a ricochet in order to get the best line of fire on the attackers.

He dropped two with clean head shots before a Soviet frag grenade plinked on the boulder in front of him, bouncing outside the rock circle.

"Hit it!" he cried, diving down.

The concussion rattled his brains.

"We've got to go," he told Lee. "We can pull back and fight 'em from the trail. We can't hold here. We're going to buy the ranch if we stay."

"You convinced me," Dr. Lee said, stuffing four full 40-round mags inside her fatigue shirt. She cracked a fresh one into her M-16. "Lead the way."

Hayes stood up, his assault rifle hip high, and cut a withering arc of full autofire over the tops of the boulders. "Out the back!" he shouted to her over the din.

Lee bailed out of the ring of rocks, retreating to the first big boulder on the casa side of the assault. She braced herself against the stone and when Claude came dashing down toward her, she sent covering fire to either side of him, back into the summit rock pile.

"Let go!" Hayes yelled, running right past her.

Bullets sparked on the stones at his heels.

Dr. Lee didn't need any more coaxing. She sprinted after him.

Hayes knew exactly where he was going. There was a solid ridge line down the path another fifty yards. From behind it, he and the doc could hold back the hordes until they caught their breath.

He could hear her footfalls right behind him, practically on his heels. As he slowed to duck under an overhanging ledge of rock, she darted by him. Before he could get past the overhang, there was a clap of thunder, a blinding wash of white light and the ground leaped up and hit him in the face.

Not content, the ground then slammed into the back of his head. Suddenly it was very hard to breathe.

20

Nanos gave the naked Indian a concerned look. "Are you all right?" he asked.

"Say what you mean."

"Huh?"

"What you mean to ask is 'are you all there?'"

"Okay," the Greek said amiably. "Are you all there?"

"How do I look?"

"Not all there."

Billy Two nodded. "Good guess. I've been on the toot to end all toots. Talking cockroaches. Men made of mist. The ultimate Bic flick. And those ComBloc goons were going to cut off my head and bring it to you."

"Make a hell of a paperweight."

"I'm serious."

"Yeah, me too."

"Get any while I've been gone?"

"Some almost got me. Can I ask you something?"

The Indian nodded.

"What's with the skin show? Did you lose all

your clothes? Or did you become a practicing nudist in Moscow?''

''I know where my clothes are, and I'm not a nudist.''

''Hey, old Chank is around the other side of the bunkhouse,'' Alex said. ''He'd really like to see you. Come on, let's give the Inuit a thrill.''

''You go get him and bring him here.''

''Sure, Billy, anything you say,'' the Greek told him. ''Just stay put until I get back. Man, it's great to see your ugly face again.''

With that, Nanos headed around the back of the bunkhouse. He opened the building's rear door a crack, then called softly, ''Hey, Chank, come here.''

The Eskimo appeared out of the gloom. ''What's up?'' he said, shouldering his M-16.

''Got a big surprise for you. Come with me.''

Nanos waved the bush pilot on. When they rounded the corner of the bunkhouse, the Greek stopped dead in his tracks.

''Where the hell did he go?'' Alex said. ''He told me he was going to wait.''

Chank rubbed his round chin. ''Where did who go? What are you talking about?''

''Billy Two,'' Nanos said. ''He was standing right where you are now not three minutes ago.''

''Starfoot, huh?''

''Yeah and he was buck naked.''

The Eskimo winced. ''Look, Alex, we've all been doing without sleep for a couple days now.

Funny things can happen to a guy's mind when he can't get his proper z's."

"I saw him. And he was naked. The bastard just up and walked off. He did it on purpose, to make you think I'm losing it. Holy shit, he's the one running around in his fucking birthday suit."

"Yeah, right, Alex. Why don't you go into the bunkhouse and have a little lie down? I'll wake you up if things get any hotter."

Down the hill from them a hand grenade blew.

"That was on the goddamn road!" Chank said, pointing to the flash of light.

Nanos unslung his Armalite. It was not only on the road; it was close.

When the second grenade went off, the two men moved quickly into their defensive positions, one at either end of the stone bunkhouse.

The Greek tried to put Starfoot out of his head. The last thing he needed was a distraction. It wasn't easy to dispense with a six-foot-six hallucination, though. He wished to hell he'd reached out and touched the guy on the arm or something, to make sure he was real. Christ, what was it Billy had told him about cockroaches? Talking cockroaches? Maybe it *was* just from lack of sleep like Dayo said?

Nanos squinted out into the darkness. Was there a naked half Osage, half Navaho running around out there? He pulled the M-16's butt tighter to his armpit. He sure hoped not.

Something moved along the edge of the terrace wall.

Nanos tracked it in his sights. Don't be Starfoot, he thought. Don't be that wacko.

A flame winked at him. An assault rifle barked. And steel-cored slugs gnawed at the stone edge of the building beside his head.

Alex pulled back, dropping to a prone position. He poked his weapon out around the corner, scanning for a target opportunity.

He got more than one.

Three Spetsnaz troopers were coming over the top of the wall. Alex thumbed the M-16's fireselector switch to full-auto, then flattened the trigger. The tight little rifle spit 5.56mm slugs at a frantic pace. He hit two of the attackers. He knew because of the slapping sounds the slugs made when they hit flesh. The third guy bailed out, jumping back over the wall.

The Greek waited patiently, keeping his sights on the place along the wall where he last saw the shadow-blur of the third man's head. It appeared again. Right in the middle of his sight picture. He pressed the trigger lightly. The weapon stuttered four times. Four polite bucks against his shoulder. Four flat cracks from the muzzle. Four hard slaps at point of impact. The head dropped away for a second and final time.

Slugs gouged at the stonework over his head, raining sparks and stone flecks on the back of his neck. Alex rolled behind the bunkhouse. From the other side of the building, an M-16 began chattering away. Dayo had something to keep him occupied.

Then building and earth rocked.

Alex dropped to one knee, stunned by the power of the explosion.

A second RPG hit.

Then a third.

Alex went down on his face, covering the back of his head with his hands.

The ancient walls began to come apart, the mortar cracking, the huge stone blocks sliding inward.

The far end of the bunkhouse took two more solid hits, then the roof caved in along with the short side walls.

Nanos poked the muzzle of his rifle around the corner and dumped the rest of the magazine, spraying the top of the terrace wall. He knew he wasn't going to hit anybody, but he wanted to give them something to think about. He ripped out the empty clip and cracked in a fresh one. Then he turned and ran along the backside of the bunkhouse as fast as he could go.

Dayo's end of the building had been turned into a pile of smoking rubble.

Come on, man, be all right! Nanos thought, lifting aside the twisted sheets of corrugated roofing. As he bent over the task, bullets whined over his head and off the jumble of fallen building blocks.

"Chank, you got to help me," he said. "Where the hell are you?"

Then he saw the hand sticking up from between two hunks of stone.

"I'll get you out," Alex told him, pulling the debris out of the way. He worked frantically to free the man's upper torso. Dayo's brown face was dusted white, his eyes closed. He didn't seem to be breathing.

Nanos put an ear to his chest, listening for a heartbeat. He could hear none. He tried to take a pulse at the wrist. There was none.

It was then that he saw the pair of pants lying on the grass some fifteen feet away. Alex rose and walked over to them, oblivious to the bullets shrieking past him.

The pants had legs in them.

Not just legs, either. Hips, buttocks, as well. All of which once belonged to Chank Dayo.

21

Barrabas ran like a man possessed. Not to get away from the troopers pursuing him, but to gain some time, some slack. If it had been a flat-out sprint on a regulation course, he wouldn't have had a chance against the younger, race-trained Spetsnaz soldiers. The course wasn't straight. It was a maze of trees that all looked the same, of terraces that were indistinguishable from one another.

And there were unseen perils.

Partially covered ditches.

Aboveground water lines.

Pieces of cultivation equipment.

They all made for an interesting contest.

Even as Barrabas poured on the speed, he heard a crash and thud behind him. Someone had tripped. And with any luck, broken his fucking neck.

When he had gotten as much breathing room as he figured he could get, Barrabas put on his brakes. The soles of his shoes skidded on the carpet of loose leaves and fallen blossoms. He stopped and turned, bringing the Browning up in a two-handed grip.

He was hoping to hell that one of the Spetsnaz guys was a good deal faster than the others. His hope was answered. A man in black charged around a tree trunk, straight into his combat sights.

The soldier tried to dive aside, figuring that he could tuck and roll and come up shooting.

Barrabas had seen the trick before. In a comic book.

He shot the trooper in the base of the spine as he dived. As a result there was no tuck and no roll, only a bone-jarring belly flop in the dirt. Barrabas stepped forward and finished the man off with a pair of close-range shots to the back of the head, then quickly set to work.

He grabbed the dead man by the back of his trouser waistband and hauled him over to the terrace wall, propping him up against it in a slumped sitting position with legs outstretched. When this was done, Barrabas took a fragmentation grenade from his battle harness, removed both safeties and laid it carefully in the palm of the dead hand. He wrapped the fingers tightly around the safety handle so it could not possibly spring off. Then he slipped the hand and grenade under the back of the man's thigh, pinning it there.

The whole operation required no more than a few seconds.

By the time the rest of the fireteam caught up with its fastest runner, Barrabas was already up the terrace wall and sitting on the next level.

"Uhhhhh!" he said softly into his cupped hand, aiming the sound down the wall at the seated dead man.

The troopers filtered in slowly, cautiously.

Barrabas groaned again, this time even more softly than before.

The troopers spoke to the dead man.

One of them knelt down beside him and gave his limp arm a good shake.

Barrabas rolled back from the edge of the wall, curling and covering.

The dead hand slipped out from under the thigh, jelly fingers releasing the grenade, letting the safety handle pop off, letting the grenade roll away into the dark. Even if the soldiers had been aware of what had happened, of the terrible danger they were in, they couldn't have gotten away. They didn't know which way to run.

In a way it was a fair exchange. The trooper had given the corpse a shake; so it was the corpse's turn to shake back. It shook and then some.

The four soldiers were leaning over their dead comrade when the grenade detonated. All four were blown flat on their asses by the power of the explosion. The ignominy of it all was the least of their worries. Shards of red-hot metal propelled by the concussive blast slashed through heads, necks, killing them all instantly.

Barrabas rolled to his feet and put some distance between himself and the carnage. When he was satisfied with the gap, he stopped and checked his watch. Then he moved on, heading for his rally point with O'Toole.

When he reached the prearranged spot, the Irishman was nowhere in sight. Barrabas took cover behind a fallen tree and waited.

It was a hard thing to do with the night suddenly full of gunshots, grenade blasts, screams. He checked his watch for the tenth time in three minutes. Maybe O'Toole had bought it? It wasn't like him to be late to a rendezvous.

Come on, Liam, Barrabas thought. Get your ass in gear.

As far as O'Toole was concerned that was easier said than done. His ass was, at that very moment, backed six feet up a centuries-old culvert.

Outside the overgrown opening to the drainpipe, past the ragged curtain of moss, the sparse fringe of weed, Liam could see men moving about.

The men of Spetsnaz.

They were hunting him. For five minutes they had been trying to follow the trail of blood oozing from his shoulder wound, trying to trace it back to its source. It had been dumb luck that he had found the culvert at all. The impact of the AK slug had put him on his much-broken nose, not ten feet from the entrance. It hadn't been his first choice for a hiding place; it had been his only choice. He had no more than backed in when the pursuit arrived. And salvation had quickly turned into a death trap.

He had his Beretta 92SB out in front of him, cocked and unlocked. The compact 9mm auto-pistol had nineteen Silvertip hollowpoints in its staggered-row box magazine. That didn't mean he stood a chance in hell if one of the Soviet special forces men decided to take a peek up the pipe; it just meant O'Toole had an opportunity to check out in style.

His wound was high on the back of the shoulder. He wasn't bleeding all that badly, but his whole arm from socket to fingertips felt as if it was made of wood. Except when he accidentally bumped it. Then it was all he could do to keep from screaming. The bullet had shattered something in his shoulder, of that he had no doubt.

One of the troopers in his line of sight squatted down and put two fingers to the earth. He raised them to his face, his nose.

Let it be dog shit, O'Toole prayed.

The trooper called over his fellows, showing them what he'd found. He straightened up and pointed along the ground, in the general direction of the drainpipe that was set in the bottom of the terrace wall. A bush-beating party was quickly instituted.

Liam backed up as far as he could in the pipe, until his heels touched a bend or an obstacle behind him. He had retreated three feet from the opening but he knew it wasn't good enough. The culvert entrance would attract more than casual attention from the searchers as it was the obvious place for a wounded man to crawl to.

And once they had found him, Liam thought, they would frag him with a grenade rather than risk a shoot-out and possible casualties.

O'Toole tightened his lefthanded grip on the Beretta. It felt clumsy as he was not a southpaw. Not that the shooting he intended to do called for finesse. The first head that appeared in the opening was going to eat Silvertips.

No head appeared.

Instead, all the legs vanished from in front of the opening.

"Oh, Jesus," Liam moaned. It was not a good sign. It meant the troopers had discovered the culvert and were giving it a wide berth.

So much for going out in style.

Liam O'Toole was Irish-American-junkyard dog. Not the kind of man to break into tears during his final seconds on earth or to beg forgiveness for his uncountable and highly diverse sins. As he lay there on his belly, Liam was racking his brain, trying to think of a way, if not to win, to at least get even.

If the Spetsnaz were going to frag him, they would do it right. They would prime a grenade, let it cook down, then lob it as far down the pipe as they could. In the narrow confines of the drain, he wouldn't be able to maneuver, to pick up the grenade and flip it out.

That was the answer.

If the grenade failed to penetrate, he had a fighting chance. It meant playing goalie. And playing right up front.

O'Toole squirmed forward until he was just inside the lip of the pipe, then pushed himself up, filling the entrance, blocking as much as he could with his body.

His first test came almost at once.

Something rock hard hit him in the stomach, then dropped to the pipe in front of him. Liam grabbed and flipped all in the same motion. He didn't flip it straight out, either. He tossed it to the side.

When the grenade exploded a split second later, bits of metal shot past the pipe opening, not into it. Shot past O'Toole and into at least one trooper by the shriek of pain that followed the blast.

Somebody outside shouted, then another grenade hit O'Toole. This one smacked his knee and bounced back toward the entrance, just far enough away to make him move, quick. He lunged for it, sweeping it away from the opening with the back of his hand. He didn't knock it very far and he had barely pulled back when it detonated with a hollow whump.

Cordite smoke drifted into his face. He shook his head to clear it.

Too damn close, he told himself.

And what was worse, somebody outside must have seen him reach out and realized what he was doing. The somebody started potshotting at the culvert opening, forcing O'Toole to flatten to his stomach. Slugs screamed overhead, skipping, scouring the drainpipe walls.

Liam raised the Beretta and rapid-fired at the muzzle blast. The reports of the 9mm auto in the narrow culvert were so awesome they made tears come to his eyes. They did not make him stop shooting. He unloaded eight rounds in the direction of the shooter, then paused. His ears, like his injured arm, had turned to wood.

He saw strobe light muzzle-flashes outside, lots of flashes, but no accompanying sounds. If they were aiming at him, they were the worst shots he had ever seen. He was the proverbial fish in the barrel and they weren't even hitting the terrace wall, let alone the culvert. If they had been, he could've felt the impacts of lead on stone through his bone and flesh.

If they weren't shooting at him, they were shooting at some other SOB. A rescuer. Barrabas! Liam thought. The colonel would've missed him at the rendezvous point and come looking.

O'Toole inched forward for a better look.

What he saw made no sense to him. Spetsnaz was firing blind and wild, muzzle-flashes coming from all sides, lines of autofire slashing through the almond grove navel high. It was as if they were trying to track a target right in their midst, a target moving so fast and so erratically that they couldn't catch up.

Liam could just make out a blur between the flashes, a shadow of a shadow. One by one the winking lights vanished.

Then a trooper hit the dirt right in front of him. The man landed on his back, arms outflung. Before Liam could aim and fire the Beretta, the unconscious body was jerked from sight. But only for a second. The trooper crashed to earth again almost immediately. From the unnatural angle of his neck, O'Toole knew it had been snapped.

A pair of bare brown legs stepped between the culvert entrance and the dead man.

"Dear sweet Mother," O'Toole muttered as he looked up and saw that it wasn't only the brown legs that were bare.

"Are you coming out of there, O'Toole, or do you want your mail forwarded?" a familiar voice asked.

22

The RPG's thunderclap caught Dr. Lee in midstride, its wind blast slamming her, pelting her with bits of shattered bedrock, knocking her to her knees. She scrambled to her feet and looked back over her shoulder.

The overhanging ledge was gone.

"Hayes!" she cried into the dark. "Hayes!"

He was gone, too.

And Spetsnaz was coming.

A hail of 5.45mm autorifle slugs skimmed the fallen limestone, thwacking into the ground at her feet.

"Goddamn you bastards!" she shouted, swinging her M-16 up to hip height. She sprayed .223-caliber lead in a horrendous sustained burst, unloading forty rounds in less than a second. Blind shooting did not satisfy her. Full of hate, she wanted to see her enemies soak up slugs, to watch them stagger and buckle under multiple hits.

It was not to be. Not yet, anyway. She needed cover to fight from. On the run, she ripped out the spent magazine and inserted a full one, then thumbed the bolt-close button. The M-16 chambered the first round in the new clip.

Dr. Lee made a mad dash for the only defensible point she could get to. She thought about nothing except her footing on the loose rock of the trail, about firmly planting each step before pushing off. Spetsnaz was charging full tilt behind her. If she stumbled, they were going to run her down.

Bullets whining overhead, she ducked behind the thigh-high ridge of limestone. From deep in the valley to her back, the sounds of combat rolled upslope. Long strings of full-auto gunfire. The hard crump of exploding RPGs. Spetsnaz was putting on the squeeze play, as she and Barrabas and the others had known they would. If they could drive the SOBs into one spot, they could wipe them all out at once.

That one spot was Ca'n Hatton.

Dr. Lee thought about the gray cubes of plastic explosive that Barrabas had ordered Beck to plant inside the ancient building and a great lump rose in her throat. What a way for her father's dream to end!

Obliteration.

Whoever picked up the pieces at Ca'n Hatton would do so from scratch, from the dusty heaps of rubble. All the centuries of inhabitation, of each successive owner first fighting, then resigning himself to living with the foibles and quirks of the casa would finally come to an end. The new builder would probably be German, she told herself, would probably throw up a chalet-style A-frame with boxes of geraniums in every window. None of that mattered in the long haul and Lee knew it. A house was just a house. She knew her father would have approved of Barrabas's plan, too. General Hatton had never played it safe, either.

She poked the muzzle of her M-16 around a corner of rock, cut loose a short burst, then pulled back. Fast. A wall of bullets smacked the stone where her head had been. The Spetsnaz attack unit had regrouped out there in the dark. The soldiers who had provided triangulating RPG fire from nearby peaks had rendezvoused with the main force. They were unleashing a withering stream of lead her way, keeping her pinned down.

Hayes had been right. The position was defensible. But by two people, not one. If Claude had been by her side, they could have shown Spetsnaz something. Alone, it was hopeless.

Despite that, she rolled to another gap in the ridge and ripped off a quick response. Again, the answering fire was so tremendous that she had to pull back.

"Damn it!" she snarled in frustration and fury, bashing the butt of her rifle in the dirt.

If she didn't retreat farther and without delay, they were going to overrun her. If she retreated farther, she could not keep the Soviet RPG teams from firing down at the top of Ca'n Hatton. They would have control of the high ground and a clear shot at their target.

Dr. Lee spun back to the gap and emptied the magazine into the dark, fanning the muzzle back and forth to cover the largest area. There were too many points of fire to aim at, too many guns advancing on her.

Slugs crashed against stone all around her, then her right arm went numb.

"Oh, God," she moaned, gritting her teeth against the pain and shock of the bullet impact. It felt as if her arm had been torn off at the elbow. She had to know the damage. Putting down her rifle, she jerked out a small flashlight from the breast pocket of her fatigues and flicked it on. The wound felt worse than it actually was. She had been creased across the top of her forearm. The bullet had slashed through the fabric and opened a shallow track in her flesh that began three inches below her elbow and ended three inches above it. She would live. For the time being. She shut off the flash and buttoned it back into her pocket, then picked up the M-16 and reloaded with her last remaining 40-round magazine.

The fire from the trail above had dwindled off. Spetsnaz was moving in for the kill.

Dr. Lee had no choice. She had to pull back. Not to avoid death, but get into a position to liberally dispense it. Pinned down behind the ridge she couldn't hurt the enemy. If she retreated, however, some of the troopers were bound to pursue her. Those she would make pay for Claude's death. All she had to do was to get them to follow her down the trail to the Ca'n Hatton reservoir, which was made to order for a one-person ambush.

She primed her last hand grenade, then lobbed it toward the oncoming but unseen soldiers. At the sound of the whump she was off, rolling to her feet, dashing past the end of the ridge and racing downhill as fast as she could go.

The trail narrowed almost immediately, becoming a two-foot-wide track of loose stones. She knew it by heart, every treacherous twist and cutback, every spot where rotten rock and a false step meant a long fall. The troopers coming up behind would not be able to maintain her pace without taking a tumble. And each second she gained on them gave her more time to get into position above the kill zone.

She stopped, out of breath, at the place where the trail turned out from the sheer cliff wall and rounded the valley side of the small reservoir. The water storage facility was almost as old as the main house. It had been built into the side of the mountain, taking advantage of a natural concavity in the terrain. It had been made in part by hollowing out the existing bedrock, in part by building up a dam of stone blocks. It served as a catch basin for rainwater running off the higher slopes and for springwater percolating through the bedrock layers. It was of irregular shape due to the uneven sides of the cut it was nestled in. Its longest side, facing the valley, was thirty yards. Its greatest depth was less than a third of that.

Dr. Lee left the trail and turned right, skirting the inside perimeter of the reservoir, working quickly over the rim blocks of limestone to its extreme rear where water met mountain in a sharp point. She scrambled up the boulder fall until she was far enough above the reservoir and the trail to control movement on both with her M-16.

For as long as her ammunition held out.

Below her the brimful reservoir was inky black, protected from the wind by the mountain, its surface satiny, unruffled. In the valley on the other side, the firefight still raged on.

I hope the others are doing better than I am, Dr. Lee thought, listening to the rocking booms, the ebb and flow of the gun battle.

Then the troopers of Spetsnaz appeared on the trail.

She waited patiently as they moved out from the cover of the cliff face, watching the shadows their bodies made against the lights of the farmhouses on the opposite side of the valley. She kept her sights on the lead soldier and both her eyes open so she could track every Spetsnaz that came into view. When the flow of troopers stopped, she started. She started before the first man could reach the middle of the dam wall.

Single shots, not full-auto. There would be no wasting slugs now.

It was shooting-gallery time.

Knock down the line of moving bears.

Russian bears.

The M-16 bucked into her shoulder as she tightened down on the trigger. Her target went down on all fours as if sledgehammered from above, his weapon clattered to the stones. Then he sprawled across the reservoir rim.

The gruesome details didn't even register in Dr. Lee's mind. All that mattered was that she had scored a hit, that the enemy was down; that a follow-up shot was unnecessary. She rode the recoil wave to her left, lining her sights up on the next man in line.

She pulled and he folded, somersaulting off the dam, down the hillside. The element of surprise was gone.

The rest of the fireteam turned back. They had to. There was no cover for them on the dam.

Four soldiers running. Dr. Lee swung her sights past the last man and leading him, squeezed the trigger. Three men running. Running and shooting back wildly.

Answering fire, aimed or otherwise, did not concern her. She wanted them all.

She got one more. The new last man in line. He

fell screaming into the water. The remaining two troopers made it back to the cliff before she could nail them.

The sounds of the mortally wounded soldier drowning, the splashing, the frantic gasping gradually faded away, blending in with, becoming lost among the staccato battle noises from farther below.

Dr. Lee took a deep breath, held it for a few seconds, then let it slip out. The bottled-up tension, the fury, were still there. She had come so damned close to getting all six! It would be harder now, even though there were fewer of them. If they decided to withdraw, it would be impossible. She couldn't go after them. If they chose to stay and slug it out, she still had a chance to ring up a perfect score. She had only used six rounds to kill four men. She had a bunch left.

At least it seemed like a bunch until the targets started to move upslope toward her, shooting back.

She fired at them but couldn't hold position for more than a couple of shots. Bullets sizzled so close to her ears, she could feel the wind of their passing. Freight-train wind. She had to move or get her head cut in two. The surviving pair of Spetsnaz troopers were showing their expertise, working in tandem, one drawing fire while the other watched for Dr. Lee's muzzle-flash, zeroing in on it. When she ducked back, both of the attackers advanced. It was a game they could play all night; she was almost out of ammunition.

Dr. Lee lay back and listened. Stones rattled downhill. Stones loosened by Spetsnaz shoes. One of the enemy was close. Within twenty-five feet. She was ready to commit anyway, when the rattling grew louder and louder still. The trooper had started a miniature avalanche. He did not scream as he slipped down the tumbling bed of rock. He screamed as Lee Hatton tracked him with 5.56mm slugs, as they stitched his body from the base of his neck to the base of his spine.

Then the doctor came up empty.

She dived back behind the rock outcrop, just in time to avoid answering fire from below. ComBloc bullets whined off the limestone, steel cores showering her with fat calcium carbonate sparks.

Dr. Lee pulled out her commando dagger. It would not give her away like a muzzle-flash. In the dark she had the advantage because she knew the terrain, the chutes of loose rock. If she could get in close, from behind or the side, she could take the brass ring.

She listened for movement from below and heard a hard clacking sound. Her adversary had just reloaded. The noise came from Lee's left. Dagger in hand she climbed farther up the hill, circling over and behind her target. She paused every minute or so to make sure she knew where the trooper was. By the time she gained the trail uphill from the reservoir, her opponent had moved to the edge of the impoundment.

Lee closed the gap on the stockily built trooper quickly, her fighting knife poised for a deadly downthrust into the side of a throat unprotected by Kevlar.

The Spetsnaz soldier whirled at the last instant, blocking aside the stab with AK butt, then smashing same against the point of Lee's chin.

The doctor saw it all coming as if in slow motion, but once she had committed there was nothing she could do. Inside her head white light exploded, then her knees caved in.

Lee came to at once, shocked back to consciousness as the cold water of the reservoir closed over her.

She was not alone in the water for long.

The trooper dived in after her. And they both burst to the surface at the same instant, their hands locked on each other's throat.

It was only then that Dr. Hatton realized she was fighting another woman.

23

Claude Hayes lay very still, his face pressed into the dirt. Everything was dark. The crushing weight of the rock spread over his back made breathing slow, shallow and painful. Over the thudding of his heart he could hear pairs of feet running down the trail toward him. Spetsnaz feet. If any part of his body was visible to them, the sole of a boot, an elbow, he knew he was a goner. With all the debris piled on top of him he couldn't have moved quickly though his very life depended on it. And while he was struggling to get out from under his burden, the Soviet soldiers would finish him off with a bullet or two to the back of the head.

He let them get well past him before he tried to move. First he shifted his right arm, sliding the load from his head and neck. He turned his face aside, putting his cheek to the earth and gasping for air. Once he had caught his breath, he started rocking his torso from side to side, making the stones slide off his back. He pushed up with both hands and crawled out from under the weight on the backs of his thighs and calves.

Hayes dug his M-16 out of the rubble, blew the dust off the action and looked downhill. Part of the Spetsnaz fireteam was chasing Dr. Lee. The rest were getting into position overlooking Ca'n Hatton with their RPGs. Claude had to leave the good doctor on her own and regain control of the high ground before the grenadiers started taking the main house apart.

The black man spit the grit out of his mouth and headed back toward the hilltop.

He worked his way around the rear of the high point, coming up behind it and its new occupants. He could see them all. The soldiers of Spetsnaz had their backs to him. They had no sentries out. No one watching for a possible counterattack. They were sure they had the SOBs under control. Besides, there were only three of them. Too few of them to mount a guard and stage the grenade attack.

As Hayes made his all-or-nothing charge, juking between the boulders, his M-16 in both fists, one of the troopers in front of him cut loose with his RPG, sending a rocket hissing down at the casa.

One shot was all they were going to get.

Hayes made sure of that.

The M-16 shuddered between his hands, sending lines of lead streaking across the narrowing gap between muzzle and targets. Slugs stitched up the body armor of the nearest trooper, pounding him back into the rocks, pounding his head into pulp.

The others dumped their RPGs and dived for more suitable weapons. They dived in opposite directions.

Hayes kept right on coming. He swung his sights on the man closest to him, pinning the trigger. The soldier fought to bring his AK up amid the hail of lead. All he did was soak up bullets in both forearms. He dropped along with the assault rifle, his throat shot away by multiple hits.

The last trooper reached his gun and crawled to cover behind a rock. Hayes didn't even slow down. He jumped to the top of the boulder, his M-16 bucking. Hayes took him so much by surprise that the soldier didn't get a single shot off. All those .223-caliber tumblers crashing through the top of his head drove the thought straight from his mind.

The hill was once again in the hands of the SOBs.

Hayes didn't have time to savor the victory. Autofire was coming from down the trail in the direction of the reservoir. Dr. Lee was making her stand. He ripped the spent mag from his weapon and reloaded on the run.

LEE HATTON STRUGGLED to the surface again, fighting the power of her adversary's grip, gasping for air. She could not believe how strong a swimmer the woman was. Not only was her upper body built like a man's, she could hold her breath so long it was as if she had gills.

Dr. Lee stared into the grinning face of the Spetsnaz sergeant, who with relative ease once again plunged her head and shoulders under the cold water.

The outcome of the contest was obvious to them both.

The stronger would win.

The weaker would drown.

Lee did not panic, even though she could feel her reserve of strength failing. She relaxed totally, then like a coiled spring struck with her right fist. On land, against an opponent in street clothes, the blow to the heart would've ended the battle. It was solid. Her first two knuckles made full contact at the apex of the power stroke. And it was on target, just below the point of the sternum. In a medium heavier than air, the speed of the blow and therefore its power was negated. Add to that the cushioning effect of the Russian sergeant's body armor, which spread the impact over a wide area, unfocusing it, and the good doctor's best shot became nothing but a love tap.

Lee grabbed for the trooper's throat again, her lungs screaming for air. If a punch couldn't help her, then her only hope was to get hold of a pressure point. Carotid. Jugular.

The Russian anticipated the move and shifted

grip, pushing her deeper under the water, wrapping powerful thighs around Lee's torso.

The crushing pressure on her chest almost made Lee black out. She fought the onrushing darkness. It was death. Jerking a hand free from the fingers of her enemy, Lee fumbled for a nerve center along the back of the woman's thigh. The Soviet trooper wasn't wearing Kevlar fatigue pants; she had nothing to protect her. Lee could hear the scream from above right through the water. Then the scissors grip of the legs slackened and the doctor pushed free, diving under, coming up behind her adversary.

As she broke surface, gulping precious air, someone shouted down at her from the trail above the reservoir. She couldn't understand the word. She recognized the voice, though. It was Claude.

"Target!" came the shout again.

The Russian trooper turned in the water to face her.

Lee ripped open the pocket of her fatigue shirt, backpedaling to avoid the woman's outstretched hands. Be waterproof! she prayed, hauling out the flashlight. She pushed the On button and the trooper's face was instantly bathed in hard yellow light.

Lee saw the woman squint.

Then came the single gunshot from above.

The Spetsnaz sergeant's head snapped to the side, her body going rigid, her extended fingers straining, quivering. In the cold light of the flash, the blood oozing from the small round hole in her right temple looked black. Then she sank slowly out of sight.

Lee dogpaddled for the reservoir rim. She made it, but didn't have the strength to pull herself out. She hung on to the edge until Hayes reached her.

"Come on, let's get you out of there," he said, grabbing the back of her shirt and pulling her up onto the stones.

Lee couldn't stop shaking.

Claude helped her to her feet, then hugged her tight to him. "God, you're chilled right through," he said.

The heat from his body helped. After a minute or so her teeth stopped chattering and the rhythm of her breathing settled down. She patted him on the shoulder.

"I'm okay," she said.

Hayes let her go and started to strip out of his shirt.

"What are you doing?" she asked.

"Put this on," he said, handing the shirt to her.

She started to argue but he waved her off. "No time for a discussion," he told her. "You can't shoot straight when you've got the shakes."

After she had pulled on the shirt and pushed up the cuffs, which extended four inches beyond her fingertips, he passed her his M-16. Hayes then picked up an AK-74 from a fallen trooper. ''We've got to get down the hill,'' he said. ''The others need us.'' With that he headed down the trail on the double.

Dr. Hatton followed on his heels.

24

Nate Beck twisted the conductors together at the charge location end of the firing wire, then trotted down the hallway of Ca'n Hatton, following the double strand of wire concealed along the baseboard of the left-hand wall back to its terminus in the casa's kitchen.

Outside, the battle raged on, moving closer to the main house by the minute.

Beck shut it out of his mind as best he could. No matter how much he wanted to be on the slope, fighting alongside the other SOBs, he had a critically important job of his own to do. Even though O'Toole was the certified demolitions expert on the team, Barrabas had picked Beck to lay the wire and set the C-4 charges in place.

Nate knew why. O'Toole was a better soldier than he was. But when it came to working with electricity, the edge went to him. He was methodical and precise. It had been those habits that had helped make him a computer kingpin. Discipline coupled with a touch of genius.

No genius was required tonight.

O'Toole had already mapped out the placement and size of the charges to be used. Beck was just following the Irishman's plan to the letter.

Beck stepped over the dozens of sets of wires laid out across the kitchen's quarry-tile floor. He located the set he was testing and touched the free ends to his galvanometer. The needle took a deep jump to the right. There were no breaks in the wire. He took a blasting cap from his shirt pocket, removed the short-circuit shunt, then hooked it up to the galvanometer as well. The needle moved hard right. No shorts.

He picked up the last block of C-4 and retraced his steps out of the kitchen, trotted back down the hallway. As he jogged along, he poked a hole in the end of the plastic explosive about the size of the blasting cap. Then he inserted the cap into the block and molded the explosive around it. He'd performed the same operation so many times in the past twelve hours, he could've done it in his sleep.

Beck's destination was a load-bearing wall at the front of the building. O'Toole had worked with Lee Hatton's father's architectural drawings of the casa to choose the blast points. Every block of C-4 was set at a critical place to achieve the desired effect.

Nate picked up the ends of the firing wire and spliced them one at a time to the leads from the blasting cap. He used the Western Union pigtail for the connection. Then he pushed the soft bar of explosive against the wall on the X O'Toole had marked for him.

He made sure the blasting cap leads were concealed, then returned to the kitchen. Gunther was waiting for him there, this time.

"About done?" the Dutch giant said, leaning on the muzzle of his M-16 as he sat with his back to the kitchen table.

"Just about," Nate said, picking up the galvanometer and checking the completed wire circuit for shorts. Again there were none.

Gunther got up and leaned over him.

"You're blocking my light," Beck said.

"Sorry," the Dutchman said, backing off.

Nate began to connect the circuit into the blasting machine.

"What do you think about our chances?" Gunther asked.

The words had no more than cleared his lips than the whole building was rocked by an explosion. Plaster dust from the kitchen ceiling rained down on them. The lights flickered, faded, then came back on.

"Jesus!" Gunther exclaimed. "Did you do that? Watch what you're doing!"

Beck shook his head. "It wasn't one of mine. It was one of theirs."

"RPG?"

"From the high ground," Beck said, finishing his connections.

"Bad news for Hayes and Hatton."

"Bad news for us. The odds in favor of our holding out just dropped by a factor of ten."

Gunther cocked an ear to the nonstop sounds of battle on the terraces below and grimaced. "At the rate things have been popping out there," he said, "Barrabas and the others should be out of ammo by now."

"If they're coming back, they'll be here any second," Beck told him. "If they don't make it, we've still got to throw the switch. Come on and help me get the blasting machine into position."

The blond giant grunted in agreement and shouldered his M-16 by its sling strap.

While Beck carried the compact device, Gunther managed the bulk of wires trailing behind it, keeping them as straight as possible. They crossed the kitchen to a door, then descended a flight of stone stairs into the casa's damp, dim cellar. With Gunther controlling the flow of the wire, they crossed the cellar to a small but massively thick, iron-bound oak door set in the back wall.

Beck opened the door and entered the low, dark, arched-ceilinged room. He reached one hand up and yanked the string that turned on the bare light bulb.

The casa's wine cellar was not part of the building proper. It began where the ancient foundations ended. Its long racks of dusty green bottles stretched back into the living mountain of limestone. It was a controlled-climate environment, cool even during the dog days of summer, perfect for the aging of fine wines.

Nate set the detonator down on the floor just inside the tunnel entrance and wiped his sweating face with the back of his hand.

Gunther dropped the coil of wires and unslung his weapon. He gave the much smaller man an uncomfortable look. "What do you think about our chances?" he asked. "Is this thing really going to work as planned?"

Beck shrugged. "O'Toole knows his business and I know mine. But we're dealing with a lot of variables, any one of which could screw things up."

"Great. Just what I wanted to hear."

"There is one consolation, though."

"Yeah?"

Beck gave him a grin. "If the plan doesn't work, we won't feel a thing."

25

From his concealed position behind the fallen tree, Barrabas saw the sudden blaze and felt the shuddering boom of HE exploding uphill. He growled a curse and scrambled to his feet. He could wait no longer for O'Toole. Spetsnaz had the high ground.

They had the low ground as well.

Bullets plucked at the top of the log right behind him, plowing through it and on into the stone wall where they shattered into hundreds of singing fragments.

Barrabas returned fire as he ran, holding his Browning Hi-Power pointed under his left arm and to the rear. He wasn't aiming the Belgian-made automatic; he was looking where he was running. All he cared about was giving the pursuit some lead for thought while he avoided a stumble that would mean a swift curtain call.

The enemy fire continued, even though Barrabas put several almond trees between himself and its source. Slugs whistled by him, slashing through the shrubbery, felling blossom-laden branches, thudding into trunks. He didn't shoot back. He didn't have the ammo to waste on tree trimming.

Barrabas jammed his pistol back in its cross-draw holster on his left hip and clambered up the terrace wall that stood between him and the bunkhouse level.

Spetsnaz was in high gear behind him. It sounded as if at least a dozen men were crashing through the almond groves at his back.

Without grenades, without an assault rifle, he could do nothing to slow their advance. He cleared the top of the wall and sprinted for the bunkhouse.

It had taken a hell of a beating. Half of it had collapsed, tin roof and heavy supporting timbers down among the rubble of the walls. Dayo and Nanos, the two SOBs assigned to defend the position, were nowhere in sight.

Autofire clattered to Barrabas's back as he got within ten feet of cover. Six or seven AKs spit death his way. Caught in midstride, the white-haired man took a slug to the right calf; at the same instant he was creased along the left side of his rib cage. His wounded leg wouldn't support his weight. As he stepped down on it, the leg gave way and he crashed hard to the ground.

It felt as if someone was ripping his calf away from the bone with a pair of ice tongs.

Still, he managed to twist around in the dirt, free his Hi-Power from hip leather. Snarling an unbroken string of curses, he pumped slug after 9mm slug at the line of shadow heads poking up over the terrace wall. The troopers fired as they clung to the downhill side of the wall. They had solid cover; he had none. Barrabas emptied the pistol's magazine to little effect.

When he stopped shooting, the troopers started to advance. They only got a few feet over the top of the wall before they took fire from another source. Two of the soldiers went down at once, thrashing as slugs slapped their flesh.

The bullets came from the other end of the bunkhouse, the slugs whipping past Barrabas's position and driving the soldiers back.

Barrabas didn't wait for a further invitation. With covering fire screaming overhead, he crawled the remaining distance between himself and the fallen wall of the bunkhouse. When he was safely behind it, he ejected the Browning's spent mag and rammed in a new fully loaded one. Then he examined his leg. He didn't have to roll up the leg of his fatigue pants to do so. He could see both entrance and exit wounds on the back and front of his calf. A clean through and through. But the exit wound was four times the size of the entry. Blood seeped steadily from the ragged hole, staining his pant leg from shin to ankle.

The sound of feet running toward him made the white-haired man momentarily disregard the numbing pain of his injury.

Alex Nanos dashed around the back side of the half-leveled bunkhouse, right into his commander's combat sights.

Barrabas lowered his weapon.

"Holy shit," Nanos exclaimed, kneeling down to look at the wound. "That is ugly. We'd better do something about it and quick."

"What we're gonna do is get our butts out of here before those bastards regroup," Barrabas told him. "Come on, help me up."

"Sure, Colonel, you can lean on me."

The Greek pulled Barrabas to his feet, then clamped a powerful arm around his waist. "Like a three-legged race," Nanos said as they began to run-hop toward the terrace to the next level, the main house level.

Barrabas said nothing.

It was hard to talk with the tip of one's tongue caught between tightly clenched teeth.

To keep from screaming.

Every time the foot of his injured leg hit the ground, the invisible ice tongs went to work on his calf muscle, pulling it slowly apart. Barrabas had been wounded in action many times before, but it wasn't something anyone could get used to. The pain, even when his leg wasn't jarred, kept building and building as the initial shock wore off, building until it felt as if his leg was going to explode.

As they hobbled along, the Greek barraged him with conversation. "Dayo bought it," he said. "Took what had to be almost a direct hit from a Commie RPG. Poor bastard never knew what the hell hit him."

Barrabas did not respond to the bad news.

And that started the Greek talking even faster. "Right before Dayo got it, I saw Starfoot."

Despite the haze of pain the familiar name registered.

"You saw Billy Two?"

"He's here on the hill somewhere. I saw him for a minute or two, then he just disappeared," Nanos paused, then added, "Colonel, he was naked."

Barrabas gave him a hard look.

"No shit. I mean it. He's running around up here unarmed and in the altogether. He's gone over the fucking edge and then some. He was talking about having meaningful discussions with cockroaches."

They reached the last terrace wall, but not before the bullets of the pursuing Spetsnaz. Steel exploded on rock as Nanos helped Barrabas up and over the barrier. The Greek climbed up after him, turning his M-16 on the troops filtering through the screen of trees. A couple of quick answering bursts put the Russian soldiers on their bellies. But only for a moment, until they gauged the severity of the threat.

"We could sure use O'Toole, Colonel," Nanos said, cracking a fresh 40-round mag into his rifle and thumbing the bolt-close button. "Where the hell is he?"

"Don't know," Barrabas said.

"Try over here," said a voice from the dark.

"Liam!"

"None other, Colonel. Sorry I missed the meet. Got a wing clipped. If it hadn't been for Billy Two...."

"You saw him, too?" Nanos said, helping Barrabas over to where the Irishman knelt.

"Saw him? That bare-assed lunatic saved my fucking life! He killed a half-dozen Spetsnaz with his hands, then carried me all the way up here."

"Where is he?" Barrabas asked.

"One second he was here, the next he was gone. Spooky."

O'Toole punctuated his remark with a short burst of autofire from the M-16 in his left hand. Nanos followed suit with a longer string of lead. Shadow heads were popping up over the top of the last wall. Heads and AK muzzles.

"Time to move on," Barrabas said.

The three of them scrambled to the veranda of Ca'n Hatton. O'Toole kicked open the front doors and then held back just inside the entryway to cover the necessarily slow and clumsy retreat of his friends.

"Come on, Liam!" Barrabas shouted over his shoulder as Nanos half carried him down the hallway. "Goddammit, you red-haired asshole, that's an order!"

The Irishman cracked a grin, then took his own sweet time to obey. He waited until the other two were out of the line of fire from the veranda before he backed down the hall. When he reached the first turn, he broke into an all-out run. He caught up with Barrabas and Nanos in the casa's kitchen. A reunion was taking place.

An SOB reunion.

"We thought you guys had had it!" Hayes said.

"Same here," Barrabas admitted. "Especially when the RPGs started coming from above. What happened on the hilltop?"

"We had a slight problem," Claude said. "We lost the goddamn hill."

"Mr. Hayes eliminated the problem," Dr. Lee said as she took a quick look at the wounds. "Let's get these men down into the cellar."

"Go for a midnight swim, Doc?" Nanos asked as he and Gunther shouldered their white-haired leader between them. "You know you're supposed to take your clothes off first."

"Too much of a prude, Alex," the bedraggled doctor said, stepping over the thick pile of detonator wires and leading the way down the cellar stairs.

Beck and Hayes were the last two in the kitchen.

"Aren't you coming, Claude?" Beck asked the black man as he headed for the open door.

"Somebody's got to stick around up here to make sure the latecomers find their way in," Hayes said. "We wouldn't want to start the party before all the guests have arrived."

"Hey, *I* wired this place to blow," Beck told him. "It's gonna blow when I hit the button."

"You just hang fire until I come charging through that wine cellar door. We're gonna get *all* these red suckers."

26

Lieutenant Skorokhvatov sat with his back to the last terrace wall, not ten yards from the first step of Ca'n Hatton's wide veranda. There had been no gunfire for two or three minutes. He held his walkie-talkie pressed tight to his ear, listening with eyes closed to the recriminations and fury of his ball-less commander-in-chief.

"Where is that bitch Ilin?" Balandin demanded.

"She hasn't reported in since her unit took control of the summit, sir."

"If she captured the summit, where is her supporting fire, Lieutenant?"

"I don't know, sir."

"That filthy traitorous bitch has sabotaged my plan. I was counting on her unit being able to drive the SOBs from the casa. Now you're going to have to do it."

"Sir?"

"I want you to sweep the place out with tear gas and bullets. Do it room by room if you have to, but I will have those mercenaries tonight. Their execution will take place exactly on schedule. Do you understand, Lieutenant?"

Skorokhvatov understood all right. He and his men had drawn the shit detail. And worse. The SOBs had proved themselves deadly, capable fighters. There were bound to be more casualties on the Soviet side before the night was through.

"Yes, sir," he said.

"I will be starting up the hill with my own unit shortly," Balandin told him. "By the time I get to the top, I want the murdering criminals disarmed and lined up out front. Ready to meet my justice."

"Yes, sir."

The com line went dead.

His justice, the lieutenant thought sourly. With all the expense and the men lost already, if Balandin didn't manage to wrap up the capitalist hooligans in a nice, neat, dead bundle, and damn quick, it was going to be his career down the crapper. Skorokhvatov wondered what had happened to the female sergeant. She hated Balandin, all right, but she would never have shirked her duty to the motherland in order to stick it to him. No, he decided, Sergeant Ilin had swum her last lap for the hammer and sickle.

Skorokhvatov signaled the men kneeling with him alongside the wall to get ready for the casa assault. The attack force was made up of remnants of the various decimated units that had been thrown against the hill, eighteen men counting the lieutenant. All had left dead friends behind in the almond groves. All had fresh reasons to seek vengeance.

On the lieutenant's shout, they stormed the last wall and rushed the veranda.

Skorokhvatov was no shirker, either. He was right up front, vaulting the stairs, throwing himself to one side of the open double doors to the house.

The man behind him was a second slow.

A burst of gunfire roared from down the hall, from the depths of the ancient house. The trooper took hits in both thighs before slugs plowed through his cranium, boring holes through which his liquefied brains made hasty exit.

The lieutenant primed a gas grenade and chucked it down the hallway. It clunked along the floor.

HAYES SAW THE GRENADE bouncing toward him too late. There was no time for him to run for cover, no place for him to go. He thought he was a dead man. When, instead of red-hot splinters of metal, white cottony clouds of gas erupted from the canister, the surprised black man laughed out loud.

Then fell into a hacking, coughing fit.

He cut loose with another burst from his M-16, retreating deeper into the house.

Come on, fools, he thought, backing through the dining hall. Come and get me.

Another tear-gas grenade hit the floor, spinning, spewing its searing smoke.

Hayes covered his mouth and nose with a

handkerchief and backed into the kitchen. From the cover of the doorway, he sprayed the dining-hall entrance with 5.56mm lead. Why were the Spetsnaz boys using riot control type instead of frag grenades? The answer was obvious to Hayes: they didn't want to rush things, now that the end was in sight. They wanted to bunch up as many of the SOBs as possible. To keep them alive and force a surrender so they could kill them, one by one.

Bullets nibbled and gnawed at the doorframe, crashing into the wall behind him.

Hayes stepped out from cover and emptied his rifle into the dining hall, then he turned and bolted for the cellar door. As he hit the stairs, he heard the thud of boots on the floor above him. It was definitely going to be tight. He took the stairs six at a time, throwing his weapon aside and sprinting for the wine cellar door.

He hit the door on the run, slamming it back against the wall, then slamming it shut.

"Do it!" he shouted at Nate Beck, who crouched over the blasting machine. "Do it!"

Beck did it.

27

Balandin broke the connection between himself and Lieutenant Skorokhvatov, thrusting the walkie-talkie at the trooper who shared the rear car seat with him. The Spetsnaz captain leaned forward into the gap between the Rover's front bucket seats.

"Hurry up!" he ordered the driver. "I don't want to miss any of this!"

The driver tromped on the gas pedal and the Rover's fuel-injected engine bellowed. With a squeal of protesting radial tires the car surged toward the next hairpin turn. The acceleration was so abrupt, the g-force so powerful, that the driver and passengers, Balandin included, were pressed back deep into their seats.

"We have containment," the captain shouted over the roar. "The main house is surrounded and the mercenaries are cornered inside."

It hadn't mattered that the bitch Ilin had betrayed him. If the sergeant was still alive, she would pay dearly for her failure to obey his orders. While the other troopers were receiving medals, commendations, promotions for their part in the operation, Ilin would be drummed out of the service in disgrace. She would lose her place on the GRU athletic team, and with it, all the special privileges she had enjoyed for so long. Perhaps she might even face criminal charges and a stay in Siberia. Anything was possible when one knew the right strings to pull.

The driver hit the Rover's brakes, skidding into the hairpin, throwing passengers forward, then to the side as he whipped the hard wheel left. He came out of the turn with drive wheels spinning, tires screeching on the tarmac.

For a blinding instant, Balandin had a vision of what was going to happen. Of his troopers jacking up one end of the Rover, pulling off a drive wheel. Of the black-haired bitch, Leona Hatton, tied to a tree, her belly sliced open, her glistening entrails lashed to the brake drum. While he, Balandin, sat in the driver's seat with the car in gear, with his foot on the gas pedal, feathering the clutch in and out, in and out.

"You do have the videotape unit, I hope?" he said.

"Yes, sir," answered the corporal sitting next to him. "The camera and recorder are both in the boot."

Disemboweling the beautiful Ms Hatton once was not enough to satisfy the captain. Balandin wanted the moment recorded on videotape, so he could relive the exquisite joy of it over and over again.

The Rover was halfway up the next straight-away when the hillside directly above erupted like a volcano. The roadway quivered as if made of Jell-O.

"What is it? What is it?" the captain shrieked over the din of explosion, the squeal of brakes.

What it was came down on them.

Whistling down on them.

Great blocks of stone bounded off the road. Bounded into the sedan. The entire roof of the car suddenly bulged inward, forcing them all to duck heads. The horrendous downward pressure splintered the windscreen with a resounding crack, sending it spraying out across the hood. More blocks slammed the Rover, caving in the hood, the doors.

Finally the avalanche of stone stopped. Balandin and his bodyguard unit tried the Rover's doors and found them crumpled shut. They had to kick out, then climb out the car's side windows.

The captain looked up at where the main house had been. His face went slack and lost its color. The ancient structure was gone. In its place was a burning plateau, a shelf of leaping orange flame. Huge chunks of shattered walls, foundations, littered the downhill slope.

There were no survivors.

"Suicide, sir?" the corporal asked. "I never would have figured that of them."

Balandin was silent for a moment, stewing in

his own fury. He hadn't figured that of them, either. Finally he said, "Not just suicide, Corporal. Murder. The sons of bitches took eighteen of Spetsnaz with them."

The captain glared at the holocaust, his jaws flexing, teeth grinding, hands clenched into white-knuckled fists.

The SOBs had taken more than just the lives of his men. They had taken his only chance for personal revenge. A revenge his very soul cried out for.

The frustration was more than he could bear.

Balandin threw back his head and screamed up at the burning ruins of Ca'n Hatton, his voice so shrill, so choked with pent-up rage that the men standing on either side of him couldn't understand a word he said.

What the captain of Spetsnaz screamed was: "Rot in hell, you bastards!"

28

When Nate Beck hit the button on the blasting machine, the wine cellar lurched violently, a crazy sideways jump and jerk. The simultaneous sound of the explosion above was so loud, so close that it was much more than a big bang, it was a physical force, a staggering blow that slammed through rock and wood, flesh and bone.

In the same rocking instant the light in the cellar winked out, plunging the room in darkness, and the SOBs stopped breathing. They also stopped standing. They were hurled to the stone floor of the cellar, seven helpless rag dolls caught in the midst of falling, crashing wine bottles, a tangle of overturning wine racks.

The concussion flattened everything and everyone.

It didn't flatten the cave bored deep into the side of the mountain.

It didn't kill any of the cave's occupants, either.

Dr. Lee extricated herself from under a wine rack and got her flashlight out. When she turned it on, clouds of limestone dust swirled like fog in the hard white beam. She played the light from face to face as the others pulled themselves out of the debris of broken glass and spilled wine.

Gunther and Nanos helped the wounded Barrabas to his feet. O'Toole sat on a ruptured oak cask between Beck and Hayes who leaned against the wall.

"Is everyone okay?" the doctor asked.

"Everyone down here," Beck said.

"Upstairs it's a different story," Hayes added.

"Upstairs?" O'Toole said. "Hey, Claude, there ain't no more upstairs! This is one red-headed Irishman who knows how to bring down a house. Upstairs is spread, scattered, smeared halfway across the fucking valley."

Gunther played the straight man. "And the guys who were up there?" he asked.

"Food for the sparrows," O'Toole said. "I'm talking about bitesize."

"As far as Spetsnaz and GRU are conerned, we're bitesize, too," Barrabas said.

"Do you really think they'll buy it, Colonel?" Beck asked.

"They'll buy it," the white-haired man said, "because they want to buy it. They're not going to admit to coming up empty-handed after the hurt we put on them a second time. The ones who survived tonight are going to be so damn glad the mission's over I doubt that they'll even stick around to poke at the rubble and double-check."

"We've still got to disappear, change IDs, the whole bit?" Hayes asked.

"Unless you want to go through this little number again," O'Toole said.

"It's time for us corpses to hit the road," Barrabas said. "Dr. Lee, you know the way, so you take the point."

The black-haired woman pushed aside a toppled rack and stepped deeper into the cave, her shoes crunching shards of broken glass. The light of her flash hit another iron-bound oak door set at the very back of the tunnel. Before the explosion it had been concealed by a stack of oak wine casks. Those casks were now obstacles on the floor.

She opened the door with Gunther's help, shone her light down the narrow passage, then called back to Barrabas, "It looks clear all the way to the chimney, Colonel."

The chimney was a fissure in the limestone ceiling of the cave extension. Wide enough to pass a man, it led through the heart of the mountain to the cliffs above Ca'n Hatton. From there the SOBs would find secure hiding places among Lee Hatton's Majorcan neighbors until they could slip off the island.

"Let's go," Barrabas said, leaning against Nanos.

From the darkness behind them came a crash and a loud curse.

Shine your light back there," Barrabas told Dr. Lee.

Pinned in the white beam, Liam O'Toole blinked owlishly. He was sucking his index finger. Under both his arms unbroken wine bottles were cradled. "Cut my goddamn finger," he said, holding it up for all to see.

"Liam, what the hell are you doing?" Barrabas demanded.

O'Toole grinned. "This chance is never going to come again, Colonel. The chance to get shit-faced at our own wake."

Barrabas turned to address Beck and Hayes. "For God's sake, don't just stand there," he said. "Give the man a hand with those bottles!"

29

Billy Two watched the sudden and complete destruction of Ca'n Hatton from the cheap seats, a boulder on the mountainside high above the casa.

He watched and felt nothing, inside or out.

He was naked to the night air, but he was not shivering as he should have been; indeed, he had no sense of cold or warmth.

His friends were all dead, but he was not sad.

His enemies had been destroyed, but he was not happy.

Of both nothings that he felt, the nothing inside and the nothing outside, it was the inside one that worried him most. For the longest time he had been filled with hate for his tormentors. It had been his sole reason to endure, to draw breath. Now that he had had his vengeance, had spilled the blood owed him, his hate had vanished, leaving a terrible hollowness in its wake.

Hawk Spirit? Billy Two thought, clutching his head in his hands. Hawk Spirit, who am I?

There was no answer.

Hawk Spirit? What am I?

Again, there was no answer.

There was a sound, though. From the valley far below. The sound of an animal gone mad. A piercing, quavering cry of impotent rage. It was repeated again and again, echoes of echoes of echoes.

Billy Two straightened up, arched his spine, stretched back his neck, tipped his chin toward the starless heavens.

And howled along.

It seemed like the thing to do.

Nile Barrabas and the
Soldiers of Barrabas are the

SOBs

by Jack Hild

Nile Barrabas is a nervy son of a bitch who was the last
American soldier out of Vietnam and the first man into a
new kind of action. His warriors, called the Soldiers of
Barrabas, have one very simple ambition: to do what the
Marines can't or won't do. Join the Barrabas blitz! Each
book hits new heights—this is brawling at its best!

"Nile Barrabas is one tough SOB himself.... A wealth of
detail.... SOBs does the job!"
— *West Coast Review of Books*

#1 The Barrabas Run   #4 Show No Mercy
#2 The Plains of Fire   #5 Gulag War
#3 Butchers of Eden   #6 Red Hammer Down

**GOLD
EAGLE**

Available wherever paperbacks are sold.

An epic novel of exotic rituals
and the lure of the Upper Amazon

THE TAKERS
RIVER OF GOLD

Journey to a lost world on the edge of time…

Deep in the steaming heart of the Brazilian rain
forest there lurks a forgotten world, a fabled world—
the lost city of the Amazon warrior-women. But as
adventurers Josh Culhane and Mary Mulrooney
probe deeper, the uncharted jungle yields an even
darker secret—a serpentine plot so sinister it
challenges the farthest reaches of the mind.

Best-selling novelist Jerry Ahern, author of
The Survivalist and *Track*, once again teams up with
S. A. Ahern to boldly combine myth and fiction in a
gripping tale of adventure in the classic tradition of
Journey to the Center of the Earth and
Raiders of the Lost Ark.

Culhane and Mulrooney are The Takers.
You've never read adventure like this before.

GET THE NEW WAR BOOK AND MACK BOLAN BUMPER STICKER FREE!

Mail this coupon today!

FREE! THE NEW WAR BOOK AND MACK BOLAN BUMPER STICKER
when you join our home subscription plan.

Gold Eagle Reader Service, a division of Worldwide Library
In U.S.A.: 2504 W. Southern Avenue, Tempe, Arizona 85282
In Canada: P.O. Box 2800, Postal Station A, 5170 Yonge Street, Willowdale, Ont. M2N 6J3

YES, rush me The New War Book and Mack Bolan bumper sticker FREE, and, under separate cover, my first six Gold Eagle novels. These first six books are mine to examine free for 10 days. If I am not entirely satisfied with these books, I will return them within 10 days and owe nothing. If I decide to keep these novels, I will pay just $1.95 per book (total $11.70). I will then receive the six Gold Eagle novels every other month, and will be billed the same low price of $11.70 per shipment. I understand that each shipment will contain two Mack Bolan novels, and one each from the Able Team, Phoenix Force, SOBs and Track libraries. There are no shipping and handling or any other hidden charges. I may cancel this arrangement at any time, and The New War Book and bumper sticker are mine to keep as gifts, even if I do not buy any additional books.

IMPORTANT BONUS: If I continue to be an active subscriber to Gold Eagle Reader Service, you will send me FREE, with every shipment, the AUTOMAG newsletter as a FREE BONUS!

Name	(please print)	
Address		Apt. No.
City	State/Province	Zip/Postal Code
Signature	(If under 18, parent or guardian must sign.)	

This offer limited to one order per household. We reserve the right to exercise discretion in granting membership. If price changes are necessary you will be notified.

116–BPM–PAE5   AA-SUB-1R

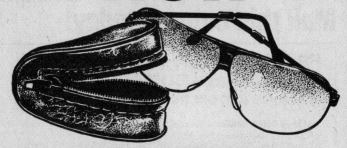